SLOCUM KNEW
THE ODDS WERE AGAINST HIM

John Slocum uncoiled from his haunches with all the strength he had left. One hand caught the edge of the trap and the other swept up to grip George Ives's ankle. Slocum fell back into the pit, but his hand stayed locked around the man's anklebone, and George whooped, tossed his bucket and lantern high in the air and came right down after Slocum.

Slocum landed on his back and lost his wind. George came down on his right side and mashed his arm pretty bad.

Slocum rolled out from under and smashed George across the face with his forearm. George reeled back and slid into a corner, but Slocum was right after him. Groping in the dark corner, George found his six-gun. He was working to bring it up and blow Slocum's lights out.

JAKE LOGAN
SLOCUM'S BLOOD

1

No sense buckin' the odds, John Slocum thought as he looked at the four guns leveled at him. His right hand wanted to buck the odds. His strong fingers wanted to jerk his .44-.40 out of the saddle scabbard and start it smoking. They trembled slightly, but Slocum showed his teeth in something very much like a grin. "Afternoon, gents. Cold enough for you?"

It was damn cold—30°, halfway up Montana's Absaroka Mountains, that December.

The trail was narrow here, winding its way through the giant boulders some ancient avalanche had hurled down the mountainside. Like pop-up targets, the four gunmen simply appeared in front of Slocum and his pack string. Slocum's big Appaloosa snorted, a bit spooked, and he patted the horse's neck and said, "Easy, girl. Go slow. Don't get yourself in an uproar, now."

The four men didn't look like road agents, but who the hell did? Road agents were supposed to be thick as fleas on the Blue Rock Trail. Slocum'd heard all about them back in Fort Bozeman.

Two of the ambush party were middle-aged and grizzled, bulky under their buffalo coats. Slocum didn't think they were cowhands. Miners, maybe. One of them was holding an eight-barrel pepperbox, and the other had what looked to be a rusty old Walker Colt. They were handling their short guns with more determination than skill.

The third gunman was a gangly, pimply-faced kid with buckteeth. He looked a little simple, just like Billy

5

the Kid. But Billy Bonney was dead, Slocum knew. And Bonney would have killed him by now, being a man who never liked to take any chances.

The fourth ambusher was holding a ten-gauge Greener like he knew what it was for. He motioned Slocum with a little jerk of the muzzle, and Slocum got off his horse, slow and easy, just like he was supposed to do. He kept his hands away from his body. He wasn't wearing a short gun, but they wouldn't know that. He stood beside his horse, patting the animal's neck and making a few soothing noises.

Slocum was a tall man—over six feet in his packer's boots—and lean, with a horseman's wiry, rawhide build. With his dark hair and high cheekbones, he looked like he might have a little Indian blood in him. But his eyes never came from any Indian tribe he'd ever heard about: They were more like a bobcat's. John Slocum stood in the ankle-deep snow, somewhat casual. As casual as a lit fuse.

He'd been riding three days—three days through the cold blue mountains, seeking out the windswept ridges where his pack string could get better footing. He was tired and hungry and didn't really need this bunch of two-bit outlaws. And besides, he had only one gold double eagle in his warbag.

The pint-sized man with the scatter-gun was wearing a big slouch bushwhacker's hat and a gray duster buttoned up to his throat. His face was pinched. He had long arms, abnormally long, like an ape's. The man limped over and shoved the Greener in Slocum's ribs. And, for just a second, a red flash showed in Slocum's eyes. Shorty held the Greener with his right hand while he patted Slocum down with his left.

"Take it easy, peewee," Slocum said softly. "I'm skittish."

The man swung the Greener against Slocum's jaw and Slocum's head exploded. Half a second later, when it cleared, he was down on his knees and the scatter-gun's twin bores were cutting the skin of his forehead.

6

Slocum swallowed. He waggled his jaw around. Wasn't broken, anyway.

John Slocum just knew he should have killed that man.

"Don't get rough, George," one of the grizzled gents said. "We ain't sure this pilgrim's a road agent. Hell, maybe he's a miner lookin' for work."

"No chance." George's crazy eyes were staring right into Slocum's. "Not this drifter. He's the one butchered those two boys yesterday. This is our boy, all right. He's been delivered into the hands of justice."

"What if," the kid whined, "what if he ain't the right one? I think we better go and get the sheriff. Or maybe Mr. Beidler."

"X. Beidler?" Slocum asked.

George gave him a nasty grin that meant yes.

Slocum had heard a few things about X. Beidler. He hadn't much liked what he'd heard.

"Hey," the kid, searching Slocum's packs, called out, "look what I found!" He was unwrapping Slocum's slicker from his lead packhorse.

"Looks like we got ourselves a gun runner. You sellin' to the Sioux, bud?"

Last summer Crazy Horse's Sioux had killed Custer and a couple of hundred better men on the Little Big Horn.

"There ain't no Indians left," Slocum said quietly. "All the Indians with any sense have lit out for Canada. They're so damn hungry their bellies are meetin' their backbones. What the hell would they need guns for?"

Slocum's logic didn't impress George very much. For a second Slocum thought George was going to belt him over the head again, but George caught the glint in Slocum's eyes and apparently thought better of it.

George's lips curled. "Tough *hombre,* huh?" He dropped the shotgun so the muzzles were pointed right at Slocum's groin. "I wonder how tough you'd be as a steer." He giggled. "I seen tough bulls, but I never seen no tough steers. How'd you like it?"

7

Slocum didn't answer.

"Guns, huh? What's he got? Maybe he's holdin' guns for the road agents."

The kid was twisting the guns around inside the bundles, trying to make out what they were without untying the lashing: "Sharps—.69-caliber, Colt revolving rifle, looks like a .38-.50, Remington rolling block. Double-barreled scatter-gun—a Boss of London ten-gauge, from the looks of it. Another shotgun, single bore. Gawd damn! Will you get a look at this thing?"

"It's a four-gauge," Slocum said. "I'm a market hunter."

George laughed. "Oh, I'll just bet you are. I took one look at you and I said to myself, 'George, there goes a real market hunter.' 'Course, there ain't no game up here. Ain't no damn game anywhere. They're all starved to death. The only game up here is two-legged." He laughed loudly. "And they're most starved to death, too."

The other men did look a little puckered around the belly, but George was sleek as a pig.

"You been fillin' your gut regular enough, peewee," Slocum observed.

The short gunman drew back his lips in a snarl and wiggled his thumb on the hammer of his shotgun. The mass of shot roared past Slocum's left ear like a locomotive and flecks of powder stung his cheek and he couldn't hear worth a damn. He watched George's Adam's apple. "Got the makin's?" he asked.

One of the grizzled miners pushed George aside and snapped, "Damn it, George, this is enough of your damn foolishness! We're gonna bring this boy back to Blue Rock and we ain't gonna bring him in dead."

George snarled, "Who the hell's the deputy here, you or me?"

The miner pointed the old Walker Colt at George's potbelly and remarked casually, "I wonder if this damn piece of junk still shoots. Suppose we could find out."

He tossed Slocum the makings and said, "Name's Jim Thiel. I come from Cornwall."

Slocum nodded. "John Slocum." He built the smoke and was pleased his hands were steady.

"You from Fort Bozeman?"

Slocum scratched the lucifer on the seat of his pants and took a deep lungful of smoke. Out here, it was real poor manners asking a man about his business, but Slocum felt he owed the miner something. He nodded.

The miner spat a stream of tobacco juice into the snow. "We're sheriff's deputies," he announced. "George Ives there, he's the regular deputy, but me and Mike and Joey, we was sworn in on account of the road agents."

Slocum was glad they had some sort of name for their job. Trouble came slower from men who had names for their jobs.

"Well, Slocum," the miner continued, "I guess we might as well go on back to Blue Rock. The sheriff'll want to talk to you. And Mr. Beidler, too."

It was a party Slocum would have preferred to skip, but he was outgunned. He mounted the Appaloosa and allowed George to lash his hands to the saddle horn. Slocum wasn't wearing any gloves. If the journey was going to be a real long one, his hands would freeze.

The kid led the way on an old swaybacked gray mule, followed by Slocum and his string. The Cornish miner rode alongside, and George and the other man brought up the rear.

Slocum leaned forward so the flap of his heavy coat would cover his hands.

It was snowing, a soft, insistent, wet snow that closed the world down to a man and his horse and a wall of white with fir trees barely glimpsed through the swirling cloud on both sides of him.

Jim Thiel had a friendly pan of a face, and every now and again he'd say something to Slocum. Slocum wasn't paying him much mind. He was letting his weary body soak up what rest it could. *Husband your strength:*

9

That way you've got it when you need it bad. He ig-
nored the miner's amiable chatter about Cornish cooking, Cousin Jennies, his piss-poor gold claim on Blue
Rock Creek, MacPherson, the mine owner who damn
near owned everything in Blue Rock, and MacPherson's
daughter, who, according to Thiel, was "pretty as a
picture but hard as nails."

Because it helped keep him warm, Slocum was
thinking about the last woman he'd had. The snow was
blowing harder, and he couldn't feel any circulation in
his hands. They were tinged blue. In a bit they'd start
to turn white and the frostbite'd take a finger or two.

Thiel pulled a muffler from around his neck and
wrapped Slocum's hands. Slocum nodded his thanks.

Three days up in the Absaroka Mountains in December. *There ain't no good reason I should be up here,*
Slocum thought. *Just another damn fool mistake.*

He'd been selling game to the hangers-on at Fort
Bozeman, but the buffalo were nearly gone, the ante-
lope were fewer and not so dumb-curious anymore, the
plains elk had all become woods elk, and the woods elk
were up in the mountains now, what there were of
them. The army'd brought a herd of beeves up the
Bozeman Trail in September. Lucky for them.

This winter was the hardest winter in any man's
memory—Indian or white. The snow hit early, banked
up and kept coming, as if to cover Custer's grave with
peace and let his old bitter enemies escape.

The snow killed the game and killed the home-
steaders unlucky enough to get caught in a four-day
blow where a man took his life in his hands going from
his soddy to his barn unless he tied a line to his front
door to guide him back. Slocum found himself in December with nothing to hunt and nobody with any
money to buy and with one double eagle in his denims.
Which George had relieved him of during his search.

When the Chinook hit in late December—warm
days, warm nights, melting snow—Slocum decided to
ride up into the mountains, where the hunters were

fewer, the elk more numerous and a couple of mining camps might be able to pay for his wares. Of course, he could have robbed the fort payroll. He thought about it. But somebody might have got killed.

He had a big doe elk over his second packhorse. He wondered how much the good citizens of Blue Rock, Montana, would pay him for it. Not much, he figured.

The muffler over his hands helped; he was starting to get a little feeling back in his numb fingers. George had tried to lash his hands painfully tight, but Slocum had flexed them when the pigging strings went around his wrists and gave himself some slack.

The Appaloosa was picking its way through shallow drifts. The trail ran along the mountainside, too steep to hold the really deep snow. It was still rough going, and Slocum was glad for the sure-footed mountain horse. A thoroughbred would have balked or slipped and both of them would be over the drop. And it was a long way down to the tops of the pine trees below. It was kind of like looking at a pin cushion from above.

He'd bought the horse off a Nez Percé. They raised the best mountain horses in the world: the hammer-headed, big-footed, agile black-and-white-spotted Appaloosas. Appaloosas weren't worth a damn outrunning a posse, but above 5,000 feet they did just fine.

Blue Rock, Montana, was a muddy, frozen armpit between two 10,000-foot mountain peaks. The miners called the peaks "Baldy" and "Niggerhead," and though the manager of Blue Rock's biggest gold mine, the Britannia, had submitted the name "Britannia" in place of "Niggerhead" to the U. S. Coast and Geodetic Survey in Washington, the USCGS never wrote back to him.

The mountainsides were bare for a couple of thousand feet up. Only a fringe of trees just below the timberline, making both peaks look like monks' pates with tonsure. The miners had felled the trees and skidded them down the steep mountainside in wooden flumes to use as mine timbers and for the crude log

11

dugout cabins that lay along the edge of Blue Rock Creek. The creek was frozen solid now, and with no water for their sluices, the miners were slumbering the winter through like bears, or working at the deep tunnels of the Britannia, building up their grubstakes for spring.

The trail wound beside the creek, and Jim Thiel pointed out his dugout and waved at the boundaries of his placer claim. Slocum wasn't paying any attention. It was all the same to him.

Blue Rock had four frame buildings. The first was a low, long building that claimed to be JOS. LOCKRIDGE, GEN. MCHDSE. A porch, a false front, a sign beside the door that announced the wares to be found within:

MINERS' SUPPLIES	GOLD BOUGHT HERE
ASSAYING	HONEST WEIGHT
PROVISIONS	GUNS
DYNAMITE	

Beside it was Mrs. Tolliver's ROOMS.

BED: 10¢
ROOM: 25¢
BOARD AVAILABLE

The boarding house was a tacky, peeling two-story structure with no windows facing the street.

The Britannia mine office was much smaller—just one room, really—but freshly painted, and the small porch was swept. A sign in the window said NO HIRING. Another said NO IRISH NEED APPLY.

The trail was a road now, 20 yards of frozen, corrugated mud churned up by the horses and ore wagons. It meandered on past the half-buried dugouts, a few tents erected on dugout foundations, a forge in a shed that had to be the blacksmith shop, and a couple of log barns that served as livery stables. So far up in the mountains, the grain for horses was sure to be expensive.

The Britannia stood above the town. The road ended at the mine loading dock. The stamp mill was running, and Slocum could hear its rhythmic *thump, thump, thump.*

A few bored miners braved the icy weather and failing light to walk beside the party of horsemen. They figured that George and his boys had got hold of something, and besides, there wasn't anything else to do.

Slocum glanced at the Britannia headframe above the town. It looked like some crazy wooden tripod or an ancient siege machine. The wood on the 10′ x 10′ uprights had scarcely weathered at all. Two flags were flying respectfully from the peak: the U.S. and the Union Jack. The Union Jack was hung slightly lower than Old Glory to satisfy local prejudices.

The town was a shanty town. Nothing permanent. Just a gouge in the face of the earth. And these miners, their log dugouts, placer pans, funny accents, funny hats and foreign names would travel on—once the Blue Rock gold was exhausted—to another gold camp, another dream, just a little farther west. The Chinese would move in after they'd gone, working the tailing dumps for a nugget of neglected gold, the odd bit of silver.

The party of horsemen tied up at Walker's Saloon. The light was falling fast and it was getting dark in the swirling snow. Slocum was glad to see the yellow light of the saloon's coal-oil lamps, though he didn't expect much of a welcome inside. The Cornish miner helped him off his horse. Slocum's hands were numb again and all his weariness was beginning to catch up to him.

George grabbed him under one arm and the kid got the other and they duck-walked him into the saloon.

There were 30 or 40 miners inside the saloon—most huddled up pretty close to the big old potbellied stove —and they all turned to inspect John Slocum.

George shouted, "We caught one of the murderin' bastards!"

13

"Mind turnin' me loose?" Slocum drawled. "I expect there's enough of you."

Some of the older miners who'd seen a few bad men wondered if there were enough of them to hold this rangy stranger who stood so still and coiled, like a cat ready to spring, but they didn't say anything, and the Cornishman cut the thongs that bound Slocum's wrists.

Slocum rubbed his hands to get the blood flowing and they hurt like hell. His face didn't change. He'd hurt like hell before and he expected he'd hurt worse someday, and if good old George had his way, maybe sooner than later.

Pain is just one of the prices you have to pay.

Slocum rubbed at his hands with the miner's scarf and a few flecks of skin came off but no big patches, so the frostbite wasn't too bad.

George had a bottle of rotgut and was swilling it down. "Jumped him, we did," he bragged. "He would have tried something, but when he saw that old Greener of mine, he just backed right down."

"I ain't the one you're lookin' for," Slocum said calmly. "Peewee over there done caught himself the wrong boy."

"You shut up and you keep shut or I'll see if I can bend this shotgun over your damn thick skull."

"Yeah," Slocum said, "you would. You're a real tough *hombre,* all right."

George's eyes glittered like he wanted to start to work on Slocum's skull right then and there, but too many of the other miners wouldn't have stood for it.

The kid dumped Slocum's pack of guns on the bar with a clatter. Slocum winced. His guns all shot true. They didn't cotton to clumsy treatment.

George ordered the kid to go off and find Sheriff Hammer. "And if he's humpin' that hillbilly whore, you just get him out of the saddle and down here. He's got some lawin' to do."

George was real excited. He was trying to work the rest of the miners into his mood, but most of them

14

were waiting for a little more evidence before they jumped to conclusions.

The bartender handed Slocum a shot. "I'm Walker," he said. "Have a shot. First one's on the house for any stranger."

Slocum nodded his thanks and put the shot right down. It was trade whiskey: grain alcohol, molasses and gunpowder. The shot scorched his tonsils and burned its way all the way down to his gut. Just what the doctor ordered.

A couple of young men were pawing through Slocum's guns. One of them was jacking rounds through the .44-.40 as fast as he could work the lever, and the stream of brass cartridges twinkled briefly in the light from the oil lamps. Winchester brought its first lever action out in '73, but Slocum's rifle was the new model, and likely nobody'd seen one before. There's something about guns that turns grown men into kids. Slocum wished they'd play with somebody else's iron.

The miner spun the rifle around his finger and gouged himself a little on the trigger. Sucking at his finger, he asked, "You think Hickok's this fast?"

A voice came from the back of the crowd—a flat, dead sort of voice: "Hickok's dead. Shot in the back four months ago. Tinhorn named Jack McCall did it. Maybe somebody's killed McCall by now, but I ain't heard about it. Hickok was never no great shakes with a long gun. He liked the revolver, .36-caliber Navy Colt, percussion."

The miners made a lane for the man who owned the voice. He walked toward Slocum, calm as the hangman.

He was a dusty man in a dusty black suit. His hair was parted neatly in the middle and kind of fluffy, like he didn't use any pomade on it. He was clean-shaven, but he'd missed a place or two on the side of his chin. His boots were shined over the cracked leather, his vest had remnants of this morning's eggs staining it and his coat was unbuttoned.

Slocum had heard talk about Beidler. Beidler was a

15

heavy-set, soft-spoken squarehead from St. Louis or Pittsburgh—Slocum never heard which. X. Beidler was deadly.

A few years back, in Virginia City, a fellow by the name of Henry Plummer organized a dozen of the local layabouts and started his own business: murdering and stealing. The Plummer gang never got rich. They robbed the miners leaving the gold camp. They robbed the immigrants arriving to stake their claims. Usually they got a watch, a gun, a horse and a couple of hundred dollars. They drank all the money up at a roadhouse that came to be called "Robber's Roost." Every now and again they'd hold up the stage. They'd throw down on the driver and call out, "Stand and deliver!"

The Plummer gang ran a modest business: low overhead, not too much risk, since they killed all the witnesses.

After a year or so the citizens of Virginia City had had enough. They formed a Committee of Vigilance. They had a motto: 3-7-77—three feet wide, seven feet deep and 77 inches long, the dimensions of a grave. The vigilantes issued warnings to suspected thieves. The Plummer gang thought the warnings were pretty funny and tacked the scraps of paper on the walls of Robber's Roost and shot holes in them, dotting the i's and crossing the t's.

One morning the vigilantes rounded them all up, took them out to Boot Hill and said, "You got any last words?"

Some did; some didn't. Plummer himself volunteered to ride off into the Montana winter naked and alone if they wouldn't string him up. They debated his proposal, decided it was indecent and strung him up anyway.

X. Beidler had found his career. He presented himself in the territorial capital before a group of big mine owners and cattle barons. He explained the vigilantes to these men. He said Montana Territory would be a much pleasanter place in which to live and do business if outlaws were hung or shot in short order. Not surprisingly, these powerful men agreed and gave him a roving commission to travel around the gold camps exterminating vermin.

He wore a Colt .44 with a two-inch barrel: no front sight, no rear sight, no trigger guard, and the trigger wired back against the frame. Slip-hammering a six-gun wasn't very accurate over five or ten paces, but most Montana saloons weren't wider than five or ten paces. And a slip-hammer Colt in X. Beidler's pudgy little hand was very, very fast.

In Alder Gulch, Moosetown, Silver City and Bannock, Beidler and his pickup crew of vigilantes had hung a couple of dozen men. For a vigilante leader, X. Beidler was fairly scrupulous: He didn't care to hang the innocent. When mistakes happened, he got real upset. When he strung up Shotgun Slade, he didn't have proof positive, just a strong suspicion. Later, when Beidler discovered the evidence had been planted by Mrs. Shotgun Slade and she'd had Slade's body embalmed in a great green jar and sold to Cody's Wild West Show, Beidler was furious. Next time, by God, he'd have to be *certain*.

Slocum could see a bulge under Beidler's coat where he carried his belly gun, and he was close enough to use it if he had a mind to.

"X. Beidler," he introduced himself. He had a pale, bland, fat face, and his eyes bugged out slightly below almost invisible eyelashes. His eyes were flat as a gray ironstone plate, and his voice didn't give away any more than his eyes did.

"Slocum. John Slocum."

Beidler raised one of his pencil-thin eyebrows in surprise. His hands were crossed in front of his belly and his fat right hand never strayed far from the lump under his coat. He looked like an undertaker a little down on his luck. "John Slocum . . . You the Slocum I'm thinking about?"

"Naw," Slocum said. "I'm the Slocum that's the queen of England."

The miners were moving away from Slocum's part of the bar. The player piano was churning out a tinny rendition of an old war song:

"I thought they would spare a lone widow's heir, but they drafted him into the army. . . ."

Beidler lifted the corner of his heavy mouth in maybe a smile. Or maybe he'd just felt a twinge in one of his molars. This cold weather was hell on bad teeth.

Slocum leaned back against the bar with his arms draped over it. He wondered if he could get to Beidler before he died. He thought he could, though the shock of the .44 bullets would drive him back some.

"I know about you, Slocum."

"Do tell."

"You a road agent?"

"Not at the moment." Slocum kept his eyes on Beidler's right shoulder. You couldn't move faster than a man's hands. No chance. And no gunman's eyes ever gave anything away. Sure, the killing sparkle was in Beidler's eyes, but that wouldn't change until he'd emptied that nasty little belly gun into Slocum's gut.

But Beidler was toying with him. "You ain't wearin' no short gun," he observed.

Slocum didn't say anything. Wasn't anything to say.

"You want one?" And there was a funny eagerness in his voice. "There's plenty of short guns in the house. I'll bet you could borrow one."

And some miner—a real helpful gent—unbuckled his pistol and slid it down the bar. It stopped beside Slocum's elbow. Slocum glanced at it: Smith & Wesson, .44 caliber, Russian. Short hammer, stiff action, a little less accurate than the Colt.

Slocum wanted to. How he wanted to. He swallowed. He was reining his body hard, but he was trembling like a bucking horse in the chute. He spoke between his teeth. "No thanks," he said. "Maybe some other time."

Beidler's mouth began to quiver. "Sure, Slocum. Any time at all." He bellied up to the bar and grabbed a bottle of whiskey. He picked up the Smith & Wesson and broke it open. "Pete, if you don't put a little oil on this gun, it's gonna rust shut." He poured himself a shot but didn't offer Slocum one. "A couple boys left here yesterday for Bozeman. Some travelers found them this morning. The road agents had buried them, but one hand was sticking out of a snow bank, like the dead man was trying to flag down the stage. Jimmy Blair and Swede Peterson. They were nineteen years old. They had their throats cut. We know they left here with a couple hundred dollars in dust."

Did this Beidler really think John Slocum would kill a couple of kids for $200?

"There've been others. Eight we know about. All killed on the trail. Robbed and left for the wild animals to eat come spring thaw. I don't suppose you know anything about that?"

"I'm a market hunter," Slocum said, his voice taut with anger. "I got an elk out there on my packhorse. Maybe some of you boys are lookin' to eat a little fresh meat. I'll take ten dollars for it."

A bunch of miners slipped outside to inspect the elk. It was a prime doe, and Slocum figured it'd dress out over 300 pounds. The player piano was playing "The Garryowen," the 7th Cavalry's tune.

When the miners came back inside, they called for the bartender's scales. They measured out ten dollars in gold dust and left—more anxious for dinner than justice.

Slocum bought a bottle of whiskey and poured the vigilante a shot.

Beidler was suspicious. "What's that for?"

Slocum thought, *Because you called me a murderer to my face and you're the first man who ever did that and lived to tell.* But he didn't say what he thought. He said, "Don't say I never gave you nothin'."

The sheriff came into the saloon quick, like he was glad to leave the blizzard behind him. He stomped his boots and brushed clumps of snow off his sleeves. He wore his sheriff's star on his banker's Stetson, right in the middle of the crown. He pulled off his long coat and tossed it to George. He muttered something into George's ear, then strolled up to the bar, scooped up the .44-.40, pointed it at Slocum's belly and smiled. He rubbed his hands together and said, "Hell, boys, let's try this road agent fair and hang him before the rope gets too stiff to work."

Slocum nudged the Winchester away from his belly. He poured himself another round while he looked the sheriff over.

Sheriff Hammer was a big man. He stood over six feet and was carrying probably 240 pounds on his big frame. His face wore a long diagonal scar that ran from his forehead and puckered up the corner of his right eye. He looked like he'd be hell on wheels in a bar fight. He was running to fat—too much good living—but he moved with a curious mincing grace.

"Howdy," he said to Slocum. "Welcome to Blue Rock."

Slocum figured he'd already had his welcome.

"Somebody shut down that damn piano," the sheriff ordered. "We're gonna have us a miner's court and hang a man."

George grinned at Slocum. He had a rope coiled around his shoulder and was working on the hangman's knot. Slocum hoped he knew how to tie it right. He didn't want to end his days suckling for air.

"Now, here's the facts," the sheriff said as he addressed the crowd. "We been losin' men to the damn road agents all winter long. It ain't safe to ride in or out of Blue Rock. Now, me and George have been lookin' for the guilty ones and"—a glance at X. Beidler—"Mr. Beidler has, too. Me and George do want to get reelected this Thursday"—he laughed; he grinned; he raised his hands over his head in a fighter's victory gesture—"so we been puttin' posses out. And down the trail today George catches this ranny, Slocum. He's got enough guns on his packhorse to outfit a whole damn regiment. Now, that's only circumstantial evidence"—the sheriff smiled a big smile to show what he thought of circumstantial evidence—"but you're all men of good common sense. I say it's evidence enough to hang this John Slocum. He says he's a market hunter. You ever see a market hunter that looks like him?" The sheriff put his eyes on Beidler. "What do you know about John Slocum, Mr. Beidler?"

"Not much." Beidler took a slow sip of whiskey. "I heard he was an outlaw. I heard he killed a few men. I heard he was pretty slick with a gun. He wasn't wearin' no short gun when they brought him in."

The sheriff seized Slocum's right hand. "The calluses on this hand never came from no single jack or pick."

"Yeah," Jim Thiel said, "but he came here with an elk to sell. He wasn't wearin' no sidearms."

A few other miners sided with Thiel.

Slocum knew he could have talked his way out of it, but his pride had taken enough beatings for one day. He thought about saying he wasn't wanted in Montana Territory—that he was under amnesty—but, goddammit, how much apologizing does one man have to do?

"Besides," Jim Thiel went on, "he didn't have any dust with him and no watches, either. He only had one twenty-dollar gold piece. That was it."

The miners' courts were notoriously sentimental, and many a killer had got loose by a sincere appeal to the sainted figure of a widowed mother and some hasty promises to reform. Slocum's mother was dead. He had a sister, but he hadn't seen her since the war. And John Slocum wasn't going to beg. Not ever.

"Well," Sheriff Hammer argued, "I say we string him up. We got one of the murderin' scum in our hands. Let's get the job done and I'll buy everyone a round before we go home."

George started clearing a space in the middle of the floor. He looped the rope over the rafters and pulled it straight.

Jim Thiel was stubborn. "No," he said. "I seen a few

men in my day. This Slocum may not be a first-class citizen, but he ain't no murderer."

X. Beidler spoke in almost a whisper: "Not much proof, sheriff. Maybe this Slocum *is* innocent."

"Oh, hell. The hell he is."

So they took a vote and some of the miners sided with Jim Thiel and some with the sheriff. Slocum looked at the dangling rope and thought about how far he'd traveled.

Beidler spoke again. "No. He ain't guilty."

And though the sheriff raged and hollered, most of the miners didn't want to hang John Slocum. Slocum suspected his champions were looking to buy some more elk meat.

Though the sheriff kept on arguing, the issue was settled and somebody pumped the player piano and it jangled out a version of "The Battle Hymn of the Republic."

"All right. All right, goddammit," the sheriff said. "It's on your head. I'm gonna toss this bad hat in the hoosegow until we get some more evidence for or against.

The miners thought that was a pretty good compromise. Slocum thought it wasn't worth a damn.

As they were leaving, X. Beidler called out, "Slocum, if you give me your word you're not a road agent, I'll turn you loose." And no matter what the sheriff thought, Beidler would have done it, too.

Slocum smiled a tight smile. "Beidler," he said, "my word is kind of stretched right now. I'd hate to wear it out."

And they took him off to jail.

2

George and a couple of young miners marched Slocum through the blowing snow to Blue Rock's jail. George was running his mouth. He'd ridden with Sherman's cavalry and guessed, correctly, that Slocum had once worn the gray slouch hat and leggings of the South. George's jibes about "dirty rebs" and "scum-suckin' pigs" didn't bother Slocum. He walked steady as he could, looking neither to the left nor the right, ignoring everything but his destination. And his bitter memories.

The Blue Rock jail was a small log dugout, half buried in the snow beside the frozen creek. Slocum guessed it'd been the home of some failed placer miner, or maybe a place where some ambitious merchant had housed a few pigs. It looked a lot like the bear-proof pig houses he'd seen along the Blue Ridge Mountains of Virginia.

George opened a heavy trapdoor on the roof and gestured with the shotgun. Slocum wondered idly how George would like to eat that shotgun, but he climbed down inside, just like he was told. George pulled the ladder up.

The jail didn't have much in the way of furnishings: two buckets, one full of frozen water, the other filled with the last prisoner's shit. The room was about eight feet square.

The chinking had fallen out from between the logs, and Slocum watched the party go back toward Walker's once they'd latched the heavy hasp of the trapdoor.

If George had seen Slocum the next few minutes, he might have revised his opinion of the tall, unsmiling stranger who'd been so unwilling to fight.

John Slocum had been caged before—at Andersonville and at the notorious Yuma Penitentiary. He'd vowed never to be caged again. For the next ten minutes, put simply, John Slocum went berserk. He pried at the chinking, hoping to find a place large enough to crawl through. He clambered halfway up the walls and set his shoulders against the top sills, trying to lift them clear. The sills groaned. Those logs weighed 400 pounds each and they were supporting a roof covered with a thick layer of ice. Slocum was sweating. The sills came up an inch or two, but he couldn't lift them free. He jumped down and prowled the interior of the jail like a caged cat—restless, seeking his chance.

He didn't find it.

Maybe he could have dug his way under the logs, given enough time and determination—he had both— but the ground was frozen solid as a rock.

Slocum thought he might freeze to death. "Well," he said aloud, "they say it's a peaceful way to check out. Just like falling asleep."

He took his boots off, set them in the corner most sheltered from the wind and sat on them. He folded himself in his heavy coat. He knew if he lay directly on the ground, the cold would kill him. He didn't want to die just yet; he had a few new scores to settle.

The jail was only 100 yards from Walker's Saloon, and from time to time the snow would gust clear and Slocum could see the warm yellow light where men were drinking, telling stories and swapping lies.

As the snow continued to fall, John Slocum was remembering one of his previous visits to Montana.

It was the First & Merchant's Bank of Red Lodge, Montana. The bank was undoubtedly the best-built structure in town. It was brick, and brick was hard to find in Montana Territory. The letter on the bank's front window was gold leaf and that interested Slocum, because gold was what he and the Bailey brothers were there for.

Slocum didn't give a damn for the Baileys. But the bank-robbing business attracts some pretty crude types, and Slocum figured he'd just have to make do.

Big Bob, the oldest, had been a jayhawker in Kansas, and he killed as quick and carelessly as another man would curse. He was big, sloppy and smelled bad. His brother, Osage, was a taciturn man with a strange grinning meanness in his face. Slocum heard he'd back-shot a man in Tucson.

24

Little Bob, the youngest, was practically an idiot, but somebody had to hold the horses.

Osage had scouted the layout the day before while the rest of them stayed out of town and out of sight. Osage introduced himself as a cattle buyer looking to make a big deposit and very, very curious about the bank's security. The bank president gave him the guided tour in person. Osage laughed about it later: "Tall man, stiff as a stick, in a slick gray suit. 'Oh, no, sir. We are protected against thieves. We had the finest Johnson and Weil safe shipped direct from St. Louis. No dynamite can broach this safe without demolishing the entire building, maiming the thieves and alerting the town.' So I ast him, 'What about daylight robberies?' And he says, salty as a banty cock, 'Mr. Smith, Montana Territory is civilized. We haven't had any daylight robberies.' How much you figure's in that safe, Bob?"

While the two argued over the amount of the loot, Slocum cleaned his Colt Army .45s and checked his cartridges. Maybe the bank would be a piece of cake, but they didn't have the money in their pocket yet.

Osage figured the bank was good for $10,000. Red Lodge was an important layover on the Bozeman Trail, and the wagon masters banked their payrolls there.

Big Bob figured they'd get nearer $20,000. The trail herds were pushing north, and no trail boss in his right mind would carry specie to pay his hands when he could have it shipped overland, waiting for his arrival.

Slocum figured $5,000 was more nearly right. Split four ways, it wasn't much, but he needed a stake.

They never found out who had the right of it.

There was nobody inside the neat brick bank except the president and the teller. Both were inside the cages. Four cages—just as Osage had reported—and grill-work floor to ceiling.

The tall, thin bank president looked up from a ledger, removed his glasses, rubbed his nose and said,

"Ah, Mr. Smith. I presume you're here to make a deposit?"

Slocum knew that fine-featured man, he was sure of it. Or maybe he'd just heard the voice. But, for the life of him, he couldn't remember where. Slocum smelled something wrong—dead wrong—and he put his hand on Big Bob's arm and hissed "No!" but Osage already had his gun drawn and was saying, "Well, friend, a withdrawal was more like what we had in mind."

In for a dollar—in for a dime.

The banker smiled at Osage Bailey and his Colt and said calmly, "Ah, yes. That's what I thought you had in mind." He strolled calmly to the counter and looked them over, and Slocum had the good sense to keep his own Colt holstered.

Next to the bank president, half a dozen men with shotguns stood up and Big Bob lost his head. He got off one round, taking the teller high in the chest and hurling him back. Six scatter-guns fired in a small space make one helluva racket. About half of Big Bob Bailey slumped to the floor—a pile of bloody rags; the other half was blown back against the wall and slid slowly down it.

"I'd hoped to avoid this," the bank president said with distaste. "Gentlemen, your weapons, please. Don't worry about your lookout. I have men tending to him."

And he did. When the disarmed bandits stepped outside the bank, Little Bob had his hands on top of his head and his eyes were scared white. Four rifles were trained on him.

Slocum was trying to remember where he'd seen the banker before. Maybe during the war? Something to do with the war.

It was a real bright August day. The sun was hot on Slocum's face and he listened to the birds hollering. The dust lay still on the street. The horses were skittish from the gunfire and some men were trying to settle them down. Slocum took a deep breath.

"Would you gentlemen care to step around back?" the banker asked quietly.

They walked through the alley beside the bank—Osage, Little Bob and Slocum. Behind the bank, a double gallows stretched toward the sky. It'd been built recently: Slocum could smell the sweet pine pitch.

At the banker's nod, men grabbed Osage and Little Bob and hustled them onto the platform. At another nod, they slipped the rope over their heads and tightened it. The three men behind John Slocum all held shotguns. They all looked like they knew which end of a gun the bullet came from.

Osage and Little Bob didn't quite know what had happened. Their faces showed more surprise than fear.

The banker looked up at the gallows and addressed the two noosed men. "You are two of the Bailey boys, if I have it correct," he said. "You are probably aware that bank robbing, under territorial law, is an offense punishable by ten to twenty years in the federal penitentiary. You are perhaps not aware that if a murder is committed during such a robbery, the crime is a capital one, punishable by death. Perhaps we should have a trial, but, frankly, gentlemen, we're all busy men with work to do. Do you wish a preacher?"

Little Bob and Osage still had surprised looks on their faces.

"Very well. Do you want time for a prayer? Do you have any last messages for your family?"

Oddly enough, Little Bob understood first that he was about to be hung. "No. No messages," he said.

"God have mercy on your souls." Somebody kicked the lever and the trap dropped, and when the rope came taut, two necks broke, that quick. Slocum tightened his muscles to bolt, to kill the banker, to get the hell out of there, but somebody whopped him on the back of the skull with a shotgun, and he had dust in his mouth and he was thinking *Now, ain't this a hell of a note* as he slipped into unconsciousness.

And Slocum dreamed. He dreamed, as he often did, about the war. . . .

Little Round Top. High above the cloud of black powder smoke that swirled and rolled over the bloody fields of Gettysburg. From time to time, a rift would open in the smoke and Slocum's snipers would hunch forward eagerly over their spyglasses, hoping for a clear shot at a blue uniform. They'd been fighting for 48 hours, and since the only federal fire directed at Little Round Top was perfunctory, the snipers went about their deadly business slowly, lazily even.

"Now, thar was a shot, Dooley."

"A right smart piece of work."

And a blue uniform would roll over, flattened of life.

Though Slocum was the best shot in the company, he hadn't been firing much since morning. When his sergeant asked the quiet captain if his rifle was all right, Slocum lit up a cigar and remarked, "Fish in a barrel, sergeant. Not much sport in that." So the sergeant left him alone. Lord knows the captain had killed his share.

A tremendous volley of cannon fire crashed and made the very earth shake. When the smoke from the Confederate guns cleared, the crew of snipers watched, amazed, as General Pickett arranged his files of gray-clad men on the plains below them. *Just like a damn parade,* Slocum thought: the officers on their prancing fine horses, inspecting the files; the long lines of gaunt, brave men with their bayonets fixed and only half a mile to march, under fire, to the Union trenches on Cemetery Ridge.

It was a hot day. It stank. The sounds of the officers and the distant blurt of the bugles traveled to the top of the low knob where Slocum and his irregulars watched with dismay.

The damn fools are gonna charge, Slocum thought. He was ashamed for their stupidity at the same time he was admiring their courage. "When our boys start out," Slocum said, "I want to hear those rifles crackin'. Every damn bluebelly you drop will be one less for our men

28

to face when they get to the trenches." He didn't add "If they get there," though he thought it.

The snipers laid out their remaining stock of cartridges. The men who had two rifles loaded both of them.

They waited for the bugle to sound the charge. There was a great stillness. It seemed as if the whole world had focused its attention on that shot-ravaged field and the slow stirrings of the men who fought there.

The Yanks were lined up three deep in the trenches. Behind them the support trench was filled with blue uniforms and the bristle of their guns.

When George Pickett sounded the charge, the gray men let out a tremendous yell and surged forward. The bluebellies didn't yell or cheer. They leveled their rifles and waited.

The first Union volley was too distant and only a few figures fell. The second volley shocked the advancing Confederates. The third was a wall of Minié balls and shell.

Slocum lost sight of the big picture. He and his men made Little Round Top sing with the steady roar of their rifles. They walked their bullets down the packed trenches, trying to kill two of the close-pressed Union soldiers with each shot. Once Slocum got three: a gunner through the head, the ball passing through the gun commander's side and exiting with enough steam to smash a powderman's ankle. It wasn't fancy. They were just pouring it on, taking just enough aim to keep their bullets inside the Union trenches, not even selecting individual targets.

They were working so hard on the Yanks, Slocum didn't notice when the rebel charge faltered, its officers mostly shot away. Later some newspaper called the charge "the high-water mark of the Confederacy." Slocum always thought about it as "fish in a barrel." Soon their rifles were too hot to load bare-handed and they ripped their shirts off to wrap the smoking metal.

The Yanks were firing and firing. And often the

trenches were lost in the smoke, so the snipers fired at their memories of the Yankees' positions.

The smoke cleared. A tall, thin colonel was leading his ragged bunch of survivors into the Union trenches. Slocum yelled for joy when he saw that lone figure laying Yankees down all around him, awaiting the surge of troops who would clear the trenches and drive the Yankees into retreat.

For about ten seconds Slocum and the colonel had the same thought: *By God, we've beaten them. Never thought we could. Courage does count for something after all.*

But the surge of troops never came. Of the 8,000 men who started that charge, only 600 survived it.

The smoke settled in again, and Slocum and his snipers fired for a few more minutes until their ammunition was gone. Then they rested. They listened to the dwindling gunfire and the shrieks of the wounded.

The image of that tall colonel never left Slocum's mind.

When Slocum came to, it was late afternoon, by the sunlight streaming through the bank windows. He was lying on a formal chaise in the bank president's office. The banker was making notations in a ledger. His steel-rimmed spectacles must have been too small for him, because from time to time he'd remove them and pinch the bridge of his nose.

"Ah, Captain Slocum. Welcome back to the land of the living."

Slocum still couldn't place the face, but he knew the banker's accent: Tidewater, Virginia. When Slocum sat up, it felt like the top of his skull was going to fly off. He was wearing some sort of a bandage up there.

The banker filled a glass from a cut-glass decanter and offered it. Cognac. Good cognac, too.

" '*Captain* Slocum'?" Slocum's eyes narrowed.

The banker filled his own glass and sipped at it. "Now, that's a sight better than trade whiskey, don't you think?"

It was, but Slocum kept silent. He was trying to figure the lay of the land. There wasn't anyone else in the bank, but from the hang of the banker's cuffs, he was probably wearing a hideout gun in a sleeve clip. No accuracy, but, close up, things could get real messy. Well, at least Slocum was still alive and listening. He took a pull at his cognac and waited for the banker to get to the point.

"Captain John Slocum, one hundred fourteenth Mississippi Rifles, if I have it right."

Not many knew Slocum's past, and he'd never been one to encourage speculation.

"Oh, yes," the banker continued, "I make it a practice to keep myself informed." He gestured toward the front of the bank where the wall showed the smears of recent scrubbing and the deep gouges of shotgun pellets.

"What if we'd come in shooting?" Slocum asked.

The banker smiled. "The cages are lined with sheet steel. The same gauge of plate we used on the ironclads. The outcome wouldn't have been very much different."

Slocum remembered. The faces of two men superimposed themselves in his mind and became one: the banker and the tall, ramrod-straight colonel. "I remember you," Slocum said.

"Gettysburg, most likely. I commanded the tenth Virginians in the peach orchard. You were, if I remember correctly, commanding the snipers on Little Round Top."

"Well, I'll be damned."

"Be that as it may," The colonel laughed. "Another?"

Slocum didn't want any more whiskey. He didn't want much more talk, either.

"I've made it my business to know most of the Confederate officers who sought, uh, new frontiers in the West. The old life was gone." He looked sad.

Slocum wasn't sad. What he'd lost he'd lost. Period. Regrets weren't going to bring it back again.

"Many men have found themselves, uh, temporarily outside the law."

Slocum laughed. He'd been on the wrong side of the law since the war, and most Northerners held that he was on the wrong side during it.

"Quite an impressive record," the colonel said. He wiped his glasses before turning back to his ledger. "A few of us old Johnny Rebs try to keep in touch." He riffled through the pages until he stabbed at one with his fingertip: "John Slocum, sometimes known as Powell, Sheridan, Curtis, Fairbanks *et al.*" The banker was amused. "You've been enough men to fill out a good-sized platoon, John Slocum."

Slocum wasn't amused.

Relentlessly, the colonel went on: "Wanted in Nebraska, Dakota Territory, New Mexico . . ." He closed the ledger with a snap. "I suppose I've made my point. Need I go on?"

Slocum waved his hand. "No difference to me." Slocum was lying. If the bounty hunters ever got hold of that ledger, his life wouldn't be worth a plugged nickel. Slocum had more than $45,000 on his head, and there were plenty of back-shooters who'd kill him for a hundredth part of that.

The colonel rubbed his nose again. "John Slocum," he said, "how would you like a fresh start?"

What Slocum wanted was ten minutes and a good horse. That'd be start enough.

"Many of us have positions in Montana Territory. We almost had Varina City declared territorial capital. Varina Davis, of course, Jefferson Davis's wife. Captain, we have influence in Montana Territory, and it will be a rich, prosperous country for men strong enough to hold it."

"And when you get brave enough, you're gonna secede?"

The colonel frowned, then he laughed. "No," he said, "I think we had that lesson beat into us with a stick. Still"—he stared at Slocum, trying to read him—

32

"old allegiances die hard. You were an officer and a gentleman, John Slocum, and in your own way, I believe you still are. If I forget about this, uh, little peccadillo, you'll have no record in Montana Territory. If I forget it, you can ride free, an honest man. You can ride under your own colors again. You can use your own name."

Slocum hadn't been free to ride under his own name since he'd killed two carpetbaggers 12 years ago. It had been a fair fight, but one of the carpetbaggers had been a judge. "I'll have a little more of that cognac," Slocum said. He raised his glass in a toast: "The stars and bars."

"Captain, there is one condition."

Slocum put his glass down. "It figures."

The colonel shook his head rapidly. "Oh, no, Captain Slocum. I have no need for your, uh, skills. I don't fear my rivals. My enemies are unimportant. But, Captain, since I am, in effect, sponsoring you as an honest man, I wish to protect my investment."

"You're a stuffy son of a bitch," Slocum observed.

The colonel smiled. "And you're a proud one. But this is no game I'm playing, I assure you." He stood up, clasped his hands behind his back and spoke reflectively: "After years of using a gun, Captain, you become too proud. Where another man might walk away from a fight, even apologize, the gunman is trapped by his skill to kill for his honor. You understand?"

"It's a rough country, Colonel."

"It is. Most of the settlers aren't very good with guns."

Slocum had to admit the truth of that. Most of the settlers were plowboys or cowhands or muckers. Easy prey for any vicious man with a six-gun.

"My condition is simple. For one year from this date, you will not carry a sidearm and you will not shoot a man."

"And if I don't like the condition?"

"I'll hang you."

Slocum looked at the colonel's eyes and knew the man had 20 armed gunmen outside. He remembered the same man leading an impossible charge against impossible odds and putting himself up front. Slocum thought about using his own name.

"How do you know I won't ride out of here, pick up a Colt and go back on the owl-hoot trail?"

"I'll accept your word, your word of honor."

The last time Slocum had given his word, he'd vowed to defend the Confederate States of America against all its enemies. But Slocum couldn't forget that brave man out in front of that doomed charge. He said, "You have it."

And the colonel smiled and said, "Thank you."

Some men had his horse ready outside the bank. They silently handed him the reins. His Winchester was in the saddle scabbard, but his Colts had vanished somewhere. Slocum didn't ask where. Six-guns were easy to get. All you needed was $15.

John Slocum never intended to keep his word. Why? A promise made to a crazy old CSA coot who'd hung two of Slocum's partners—what did it signify?

But somehow he never got around to buying another Colt. He rode fence for the Sanderson spread until the ground froze—$40 a month. Mostly he rode alone, mending fence, rounding up strays, holing up in the line shacks at night. Every two weeks he'd ride into Pony with the rest of the crew.

Ever since Slocum was 15 years old he'd worn a six-gun on his hip. It was the first thing he put on in the morning after his pants, and he'd slept with the lump of a Colt under his head every night. So now he didn't quite know what to do with his hands—hands so accustomed to the presence of the gun. Tricks he'd learned long ago suddenly seemed awkward to him and unreasonable. Long ago, for instance, he'd learned to roll his smoke left-handed and light it the same way. Now every time he rolled a smoke, his right hand hung stiff

34

and ready and it felt like an extra part of his body. On those weekend excursions into Pony, he still sat with his back to a wall, and gun or no gun, none of the other waddies gave him any trouble. One look into the smoldering eyes of the lanky, weather-beaten rider was enough. The other cowpokes gave him plenty of room.

Though Slocum was a better than fair hand at poker, he didn't dare gamble. In the West, sometimes even a royal flush needed old Sam'l Colt to guarantee it.

One payday night, a broken-nosed older cowboy off the Wallace spread started picking a fight with a kid off Chisholm's drive, talking about "Tex-i-cans" and "Mex-i-cans."

Slocum was having a quiet drink at the bar when his body sent him the message that the old reassuring weight on his hip was absent. Though he wasn't involved in the dispute, the sweat started trickling down his arms. He felt naked as a baby.

He left the saloon before the big talk progressed to gunplay, though he heard four shots as he mounted his horse, patted the stock of his Winchester and rode west toward the Yellowstone.

He made camp that night by the junction where the Madison runs into the Yellowstone, a day's ride out of Fort Bozeman.

He grained his Appaloosa and watered it before he spread his own blanket roll and leaned back against his saddle. He'd killed a couple of prairie chickens that afternoon and now he plucked them, split them with his bowie, rolled them in flour and fried them up in some melted fatback. His coffeepot on the boil—just one handful of Arbuckle's finest coffee.

John Slocum was at peace. He never felt alone in the wilderness.

The stars came out. It was September and he watched a meteorite shower—brief streaks of light diving to the ground.

He'd killed the prairie chickens by firing the Winchester one-handed under his horse's neck. And he

35

was a little ashamed of that. He'd taken the tops of their heads off while hanging under the belly of his horse.

Showin' off like a damn kid, Slocum thought angrily. *I could have stopped and potted those birds without raisin' a sweat. But no. I got to get the horse all lathered up for nothin'. John Slocum, you're bein' a damn fool.* He tossed his smoke into the fire. *There's no reason to go on with this. You're poor—and you don't like bein' poor. You can't gamble, you can't hold up a bank, you can't touch a payroll. Maybe you ought to get into some other line of work, where folks are a little more . . . dainty. Sell oil wells that don't exist and railroads that never left the imagination. Hell, that's the way. Get rich, get fat, get to be senator. Learn to steal without puttin' your life on the line. Or break your word of honor. And it wasn't like that word of honor was freely given, no sir.*

But, though Slocum cursed, he was stuck with it.

The next day, at Fort Bozeman, he got work butchering. The milling herd of cattle, the chute where they killed them, the skinning tripods, the block and tackles, the salt tables, the barrels—the U.S. Army was getting its beef ready for the long Montana winter.

Slocum worked the butchering tripod, along with a rheumy-eyed old man who'd been a buffalo hunter, and a towheaded kid of 17 or so. They cut for 48 hours straight, quartering the beeves. The buffalo hunter was fast and had a dead accurate touch with his stubby skinning knife, but he was 70 if he was a day, and after a day and a half he tired and Slocum had to take up the slack. The kid was strong and willing, but he hadn't used a knife that much before and he was slow and fell behind. The three of them were red, like they'd been painted. Their clothes dyed red, their hair matted and crusted with blood, they hurried around the beeves that kept coming at them from the skinning crew. Slocum stopped just long enough to get a drink from the bucket the water boy brought around. Twice he picked out a good-looking liver and ate that to fuel himself.

At dawn they quartered their last beef and the salt crew took the meat over to the salting tables. Slocum looked up at the sky: It was going to be a scorcher. The old man slumped on the ground like a red clay statue. The kid was trying to clean his face in the water bucket, but the water was tinged with blood and it looked like the kid's face was leaking pink.

The army quartermaster came around and paid them each eight dollars. He said it was a good piece of work and the U.S. Army sure appreciated their pitchin' in and lendin' a hand.

Eight dollars' worth.

Wearily, stiff-jointed, Slocum walked down to the cattle tank with a bar of harsh lye soap. Most of the mud had settled to the bottom and Slocum dove into a pool of clear green. It felt real good.

He washed his clothes on the edge of the tank while the rest of the crew splashed around and thought up obscenities to hurl at one another. Slocum put his clothes back on. They'd dry on his body.

The old man was still sitting where he'd dropped. He'd daubed at the blood on his face but hadn't made much of a job of it.

"You feelin' all right, old-timer?"

The old man's eyes were blue under the blood-stained eyebrows. "I feel like shit warmed over. What the hell you think I feel like?"

"Get yourself some grub, some shut-eye."

The old man stood up. He staggered but caught himself. "Naw," he snarled, mad clean through. "I had enough. I'm too old for this damn stuff anymore. Time was I could work with any man and pull my share, but now a green kid can keep up with me. I got a sister in St. Joe. She said to me, 'Charlie, you can live under my roof once you quit your ramblin' ways.' Well, I done quit."

Slocum had to smile at the old banty rooster. It

amused him to think of the old frontiersman blundering around a respectable lady's parlor.

"I need a grubstake," the old man announced. "I sure as hell ain't gonna *walk* all the way back to St. Joe, though, by God, I walked most of the way out here thirty years ago. You wouldn't know about that, though, would you, young fella?" His blue eyes glared at Slocum.

Slocum knew.

"Eight damn cartwheels ain't gonna get me very far," the bloody old man announced. "Want to buy my gun?"

Slocum had just eight dollars to his name.

The oldster hobbled over to his gear and rummaged around until he found a Colt .38 Bisley. He pushed it at Slocum. "Eight bucks," he said. "I know you got eight bucks on you. Damn gun's worth fifty."

It was a beautiful gun. Old Sam'l designed the Bisley for the target matches in England while he was still making the London Colts over there. Up to the cylinder, the gun was the same as the Colt Army, but behind it the grip was different—higher, more of a fishtail grip. The hammer was stubbier and broader, and the Colt factory put their match-grade barrels on the Bisley.

Slocum leveled it and it was like he held a feather in his hand, like his hand had an extension, like his hand was ready to *hurl* the bullets. He spilled the cartridges out and tried the hammer. Smooth as glass. He didn't try the hammer, because you could shear a Colt hammer dry firing it.

"Take a shot," the old man urged. "If you don't buy the gun, just give me two bits for the ammunition. Fair enough?"

Slocum walked over to the pile of skulls and cattle entrails. The fort Indians were already picking through them for tonight's supper.

He set a skull on a post. Nothing behind it but western air and miles of emptiness.

Normally, pistol fights occurred under 50 feet. Slocum paced off 100 yards. In one of Hickok's gunfights, Wild Bill's opponent had started blazing away at 230 feet. (They'd measured the distance afterward.) With bullets whining past him, Wild Bill had coolly rested his .36 Navy on a corral post and nailed the gent between the antlers.

Slocum took a two-handed grip. The Bisley's recoil was a little different from that of the Peacemakers he'd owned. The Bisley bucked straight up instead of up and to the right, but the gun settled down in his hand real nice after each shot, like it was digging itself in. And the trigger was like breaking a tiny glass rod. Absolutely crisp.

At 100 yards, he took the longhorns off the skull with five shots. "Nice gun," he told the old man.

"You're damn right it's a nice gun." Since Slocum wasn't reaching for his wallet, the old man groaned and went back to his gear and brought out a long gun. It was wrapped in a soft deerhide scabbard with Indian beadwork on the sides. Reluctantly, he showed Slocum a .69 Sharps. It had the leaf rear-sights and hooded front-sight of the buffalo-hunter model. The leaf sights were made by Auerbach.

"This used to be one of Jim Beckett's guns," he said. "I bought it from him when he was down on his luck, in '18 and '69."

A single-shot rifle. Extremely accurate over a very long distance and with a punch like a locomotive. Big single hammer, brown octagonal barrel—and somebody had set brass studs in the butt for decoration. Beckett, most likely.

Slocum bought the Sharps. For the next few weeks he hunted and sold meat to people at the post. He bought himself two packhorses and a few more guns. He was doing all right until the cold weather set in and he couldn't find game, no matter how hard he looked.

One night, after four days of hunting, he rode into the fort with two snowshoes and a small partridge. He hadn't seen elk or mule deer for a month. He sold the snowshoes for a buck apiece, got four bits for the partridge and bought himself a bottle. He drank it, leaning back against his saddle in the livery stable. He thought he knew where he'd go next: Blue Rock, Montana.

Slocum was damn cold. He sat in the corner of the dugout jail, teeth chattering. Even with his butt up off the floor and the heavy buffalo coat tucked around him like a 20-pound blanket and his Stetson pulled down as low as it could go, he was going to freeze to death by morning. He'd slept for a couple of hours, but his own shivering had awakened him from his fragmented, crazy dreams.

By pacing the floor, he could stay warm enough, but when exhaustion set in and he'd burned up what little fuel was in his belly—just about dawn, when it was coldest—he'd drift off into the long sleep: So he sat there and shivered. If it got real bad, he'd get up and walk, but he was holding that off as long as he could.

The wind had died down and the full moon cast its light on cold, white, untrammeled snow. That snow seemed to have a life of its own, breathing cold right into Slocum's bones.

Blue Rock was quiet. The saloon was still. Nobody stirred but an old hoot owl, calling quiet while it digested its mouse meal on some roof peak somewhere.

Through the chinks in the logs, Slocum watched a bull's-eye lantern swinging toward him. When the lantern got close enough, he could see that George Ives was carrying it.

George had a little trouble getting up on the roof. He was carrying something awkward for him to handle. The night was crystal clear. Slocum heard George's wheezing breath and the jingle of the keys as he fumbled with the old doorwarden padlock.

He grunted as he heaved the trap open against the ice frozen in the hinges.

There was a square of moonlight over Slocum's

head. He could see the moon sailing by, untroubled and serene.

The beam of the bull's-eye lantern found him. George giggled. He coughed and that sort of ruined his giggle, so he gave it up.

"John Slocum," he whispered. His voice was the voice people use to bring their kids to a surprise birthday party. "Howdy there, John." The voice you use to persuade an unruly horse to accept the bit in its mouth. "I hear you're a bad hat, John. I hear you done rode the owl-hoot trail. I heard you done some wicked things in your day. Well, ain't that somethin'." And he tossed a full bucket of creek water over John Slocum's head.

George laughed like a wild dog laughs at the moon: high, shrill and triumphant. "Oh, hell, John. Now, why'd you go and do a thing like that for? You'll likely catch your death, wet as you are."

Slocum's hat was on the floor. He could feel his hair stiffening already. A good bit of water had got down the front of his buffalo coat and soaked it. His socks were wringing wet.

The floor of the dugout was slick for a few seconds before it froze. Slocum's socks froze to it. His eyelashes were white with ice, and his heart was pumping adrenalin so fast he didn't trust himself to speak. He let out a tremendous roar and jumped for the edge of the trap. But the 12-foot ceiling was too far away.

Through his spiked eyelids, Slocum saw George standing far above him, laughing like to split a gut, laughing so hard he had to catch himself or he would have fallen into the pit with Slocum. The bull's-eye lantern roamed all over the dugout, catching flashes of ice everywhere it touched.

The laughter was thundering in Slocum's ears. His coat was stiffening up already and he couldn't feel his feet.

"Jesus, John," George jeered. "You know I'd be happy to stay here and watch you freeze to death. I'll come back later. It's a bit too chilly for me and I'm afraid I'd catch a cold."

The trapdoor closed with a whump, and a few drifting strands of snow kissed Slocum's frozen face.

He didn't watch the lantern going away. He didn't hear George's whistling. He overturned the frozen water bucket and had his feet in his hands, rubbing furiously. He kept twisting his shoulders and chest inside the buffalo coat to generate a little heat. After he wrung out his socks, the material turned crusty-icy under his hands, and once back on his feet, they bonded to his skin. He pulled on his boots and jumped up and down, and nearly cried out it hurt so much, and it was hard to keep his balance when he had no feeling in his feet. Slocum reeled all around that pit, stumbling, dancing, beating his legs, slapping himself.

He fought well, churning heat from his body to combat the −20° cold and the water that froze to him as soon as he stopped heating it up. But it was a losing battle. Like a crazed athlete doing calisthenics, he kept at it for an hour, an hour and a half. His eyes were getting dim. He was seeing double. His ears were filled with roaring, and what parts of his body weren't hurting were frozen.

He almost didn't hear the girl's whisper: "Hey, you. Hey, you. Pssssst."

At first she wasn't much more than a shape against the logs. When he knelt by a hole in the chinks, he couldn't see much of her face through the narrow aperture. Just her eyes—sad brown eyes—and her nose —an urchin's snub nose. And her forehead, young and unlined, below the curl of her red woolen shawl.

"How you feelin'?" she asked.

From her voice, Slocum guessed she wasn't much more than a child. "Mighty fine," he rasped. He tried to catch his breath, hacked, spat and said, "But I wish I was in the Land of Cotton."

"Jeez, mister," the girl said, "you're all wet. How'd

42

you get all wet? Wet as you are, you'll never see the sunrise."

"It rained."

"Georgie? Georgie pour water on you?"

Slocum was shivering again and didn't trust his voice. She had remarkable brown eyes—hurt and strangely innocent, like the eyes of a shot doe.

"Here," she said, "I brought you somethin'." She had some sort of stoneware crock. Slocum couldn't see much of it through the four-inch chink, but it smelled like heaven. "Now"—she drew back and measured the crock—"I forgot about that. How'm I gonna get this stew inside? Old Georgie's got the key to the trap and I don't see where there's room to get this crock through these holes nohow."

The smell of the stew had penetrated all the layers of Slocum's freezing clothing and stopped his shivering dead.

"I know," she said. "I got a long spoon here. I'll just load her up with stew and pass it through the logs. I'll feed you"—she giggled—"just like my mam fed me when I was a baby girl."

Slocum didn't feel real choosy. "Get on with it, girl," he said.

And she spooned him hot elk meat and pieces of turnip and chunks of carrot, all covered with heavy brown gravy.

Limb by limb, his body was grateful. The warmth spread through him like stepping from the shade into the hot sun.

While she fed him, she talked: "Name's Opal, Opal Hevener, but most everybody calls me 'the kid' except Miss MacPherson. She calls me 'Opal.' I been down here before. It was August. Sheriff Hammer put me down here for three days. It wasn't too bad because the dugout was cool, you know, but the flies were buzzin' round that old slop bucket like to drive me crazy. Flies are all dead now, I expect. I hated it. He put me down here 'cause I didn't want to roll around

43

with him and he wanted me to powerful bad. I didn't have no money, so I had to turn to somebody, but I wish it hadn't been him. He's fat and he's heavy. He hurts me down there."

Slocum had his face pressed against the frozen, splintery logs and he drank in her story along with the stew and the sight of her flashing brown eyes. Already the strength was draining back into his body.

The girl pushed spoonful after spoonful into his mouth and kept talking—about her home in Tennessee; about how the smallpox had taken her kin on the way west except her brother, who'd found work at Blue Rock and been killed when an untimbered tunnel collapsed on him. "Well," she observed when Slocum was full and the pot was empty, "it's a tough world, all right." Slocum detected a curious satisfaction in her voice. "Mr. Slocum, it's a long, long road to Jordan. I hope you'll keep till mornin'. I got to git. If Georgie or the sheriff catches me here, they'll kill me like as not."

And she was gone.

Slocum hunkered up to the space between the logs, watching for George Ives. Waiting, patient and still as a Crow Indian on a horse-stealing raid. Only his eyes moved for an hour or so, and though his body was still cold, the grub was sending little warm currents from his center. He was cold, but he wasn't dead— and wouldn't be until they planted him. Even then, they'd have to put a boulder on the coffin lid to keep him down. That's what he was thinking.

George's lantern cut a yellow path through the soft blue light of the moonlight on the snow. Slocum heard every footstep as the deputy approached. He was singing: "Peas, peas, peas, peas. Eating goober peas. Goodness how delicious, eating goober peas."

When George was near, Slocum removed his coat and boots and arranged them over the two buckets to look like a seated man. He set his frozen hat on top of the coat. It wasn't much of an illusion, but it would have to do. Slocum withdrew behind the lip of the trap and coiled down on his haunches, like a timber rattler coils. He had one knuckle on the frozen floor, but he didn't feel the cold.

George's feet were kicking away the snow on the roof. "Peas, peas, peas, peas, eating goober peas . . ." He heaved the trapdoor back and it fell with a thud. He opened the bull's eye on his lantern and stepped closer to get a good look at the frozen corpse below. Just in case, he had another bucket of water.

George's left leg was only two inches from the edge of the trap and he was leaning forward slightly when Slocum sprang.

He uncoiled from his haunches with all the strength he had left and he seemed to drift upward, upward, until one hand caught the edge of the trap and the other swept up to grip George's ankle. Slocum feel back into the pit, but his hand stayed locked around the man's anklebone, and George whooped, tossed his bucket and lantern high in the air and came right down after Slocum.

The fall took something out of both of them. Slocum landed on his back and lost his wind. George came down on his right side and mashed his arm pretty bad.

The two men got up slowly, eyeing each other in the light that trickled into the cabin through all the walls. Neither spoke. What was there to say?

Ives's gun was on his right hip. When he figured his arm could handle it, he made his play.

He was wrong. He wasn't near fast enough, and Slocum slammed into him like a runaway bull. Ives went down on the ice and the gun went flying.

George had great strength in his shoulders. He threw his fists at Slocum fast as he could, but Slocum brushed the blows aside like so many flies. He began hammering at Slocum's face, but Slocum had the deputy around the waist and now he lifted him off his feet and spun him round and round, like a kid playing crack-the-whip. Then he turned the deputy loose. Ives landed solidly against the wall but got to his feet real quick and pushed off, his boot catching Slocum's hip and spinning him half around. George fell on him, yanking his hair back and clawing for his eyes.

Slocum bit his hand—bit down like he was cracking an old marrow bone—and George screamed and yanked his hand away.

Slocum rolled out from under and smashed George across the face with his forearm. George reeled back and slid into a corner, but Slocum was right after him. Groping in the dark corner, George had found his six-gun. He was working to bring it up and blow Slocum's lights out.

Slocum grabbed George's gun arm. George had plenty of muscle; when they were arm wrestling at Walker's Saloon, not many men could put George Ives's knuckles to the wood. And Slocum was half frozen to death. But Slocum shook him.

George was punching at him, gouging at his face and neck. He ran his boots down Slocum's shin onto his bare feet. Slocum shook George's gun arm, pressed it to the floor and smashed George's knuckles against the ice until he screamed and let go of the gun. Slocum scooped it up, back-handed George across the jaw, and George passed out.

It took five minutes for Slocum to get to one knee and another five to get both his legs under him. He thumbed back the hammer of George's Colt. The man's face was lopsided and puffy, but he was still breathing. Slocum aimed the Colt at George's right eye. He lowered the gun and stuck it in his belt. He sighed.

Slocum had a happy thought: *I promised I wouldn't shoot nobody, but I never promised not to turn his head off.*

He was kneeling beside George Ives's head when a voice stopped him. It was a quiet, cultivated voice with some sort of Limey accent. "My God," the voice said. "Just like two pit bulldogs."

A man was on the roof. Though Slocum's eyes

46

weren't all they should be, he could see him well enough.

"Pharoah MacPherson," the man introduced himself. "Nice to meet you. I'll just slide this ladder down and you can climb out of there—if you can manage it."

"I can," Slocum heard himself say.

"Quite good. Remarkable. I'm having you released, don't you know. Say, would you mind dragging that scut George Ives with you? I'd like to help, but I'm afraid I can't. I have an infirmity."

3

Infirmity or no, if MacPherson hadn't snatched Slocum's arm at the top of the ladder, Slocum couldn't have finished the climb. On top, he was weaving and MacPherson steadied him.

"You do look a little worse for wear," MacPherson cheerfully observed. He peered down at George, crumpled against the frozen floor. "But you ought to see the other bloke," he said. "Haw, haw, haw."

He dusted at Slocum's shirt like he was trying to brush the blood away. "We'll have to get you inside, man, before you turn blue." His face was worried as he considered the unconscious deputy. "I don't know what we shall do with him," he said. He shook his head. "You're in no condition to haul up the trash and"—he rapped his leg with his knuckles—"I've got this wooden peg, you see."

"He ain't dead," Slocum said. "Let him get out on his own."

MacPherson shot him a quick glance. "Come now, Mr. Slocum, that's unchristian. Decidedly unchristian." He sighed. "I suppose if I notify the sheriff, he'll muster up assistance."

Slocum didn't give a damn. When he stepped down off the low roof, his legs nearly gave way.

MacPherson clambered down with the agility a man acquires after living with an old, understood injury.

Slocum smiled. MacPherson probably could have hauled up George; he just didn't want to soil his hands.

Pharoah MacPherson was a short, skinny man who walked like he had a ramrod welded to his spine. His face was loose and amiable underneath his fur hat, and as they passed through deserted Blue Rock, he kept up a cheerful chatter. Slocum responded with grunts.

MacPherson slipped and went to one knee. He rose and asked, "Mr. Slocum, what do you think of the ski? I've often thought a shortened version of the Norwegian ski on the end of my peg would help me to navigate better during the winter months. The town blacksmith says I should put a spike, like a marlinspike, on the tip, but I favor the ski. The spike would surely give me more adhesion, but what if I were to punch through the ice? I'd be stuck. Rather too much adhesion, if you catch my drift."

They passed Walker's Saloon. Slocum's horses weren't where he'd left them. The street was bare, the hitching rail was empty and the snow was blowing in nervous little gusts. Slocum hoped somebody'd grained the Appaloosa and his packhorses. They'd need a good ration to shake off this cold.

If Slocum didn't get warm pretty quick, his body was going to drop him on his face. He'd been running on pure adrenalin and was starting to shake as the last of it drained out of his system.

Perhaps MacPherson realized Slocum's condition, for he was setting a pretty quick pace, wooden leg or no wooden leg.

The mine manager's house was just uphill from the tall frozen workings of the Britannia. The mine headframe was rimed with ice and glittered like a Druid symbol in the moonlight. The ruts in the road got deeper the closer they got to the mine yard. It was hard walking.

The house was a frame building with an overhanging

roof line, gabled windows and—something Slocum hadn't seen since Denver—small stained-glass panels set above the door. Slocum used the handrail to pull himself up the long stairs. MacPherson considered helping Slocum along but thought better of it when he saw the ferocity in Slocum's eyes.

A woman opened the door when their boot heels rang on the porch. Slocum didn't pay her any mind. He was looking past her to the warmth within.

Inside, Slocum waited for the room to stop spinning around him.

A woman's voice: "Don't sit him on the chaise, uncle. Here, he can use this wooden chair."

When Slocum's eyes focused, he saw a tall woman with dark hair drawn tight against her skull in a bun, and strong, aquiline features. Opal Hevener was there, too, in her ragamuffin costume. She wanted to know if Slocum had hurt George.

"I hope so," Slocum said.

"Opal," the dark-haired woman ordered, "check the water on top of the stove. My bath is fairly hot, and he needs it worse than you do."

Pharoah MacPherson was off to notify Sheriff Hammer. "Have to keep good relations with the natives, don't you know."

The dark-haired woman plucked at Slocum's torn shirt, and maybe he gave her a look or shrugged her off, because she said, "Mr. Slocum, if you don't have frostbite already, it's God's own mercy. If you don't get in that warm tub, it'll be your own damn stupidity."

Still blurry, Slocum let her pull the ruined shirt off his aching arms.

They were in the parlor of a half-finished house. The rug was down, and the varnished wainscoting caught the light from the kerosene lanterns and cast it back in a soft glow. The drapes were deep purple. A cook stove was placed in front of the formal fireplace and a tub of wash water was boiling away on top of it. Boxes and crates were everywhere.

Opal was topping off the galvanized bathtub with boiling water.

"I hope you don't mind a secondhand bath," the dark-haired woman said. "No, of course you don't. It would be very foolish to heat up fresh water when what you need is immediate warmth."

She was tugging at his pants. Slocum didn't much care for the idea and showed it.

She got exasperated. "Mr. Slocum, you won't be the first, uh, stallion I've seen and I don't expect you'll be the last."

He unbuckled his own pants and dropped his tattered gray long johns.

The dark-haired woman didn't pay him any mind, but Opal checked him out pretty good and blushed. She took his old clothes away to be burned. She thought she might find some new duds to cover him.

The bath was very, very hot.

"Come now, Mr. Slocum, let's not shilly-shally around."

He eased himself into the hot water, and before he'd got used to it, she dumped another kettle full of scalding water into the bath.

"Damn! You tryin' to boil me?"

"Mr. Slocum, your flesh is variously blue, black and white. I wish to see you all red, like a boiled lobster. Here." She handed him a cup of something.

He took a sip and coughed and the warmth spread from his throat down to his toes. Brandy and hot tea. He worked on it for a while. His body was steaming in the hot tub and some fragrance of the woman's perfume remained in the water. Slocum was surrounded by the steam and the fragrance and it felt real good.

The cook stove was one of those ornate, chrome-plated models with warming ovens on top and footrests beside the fire. The woman poured another teapotful of boiling water into his lap.

She stuck out her hand, direct as a man. "Mr. Slocum, I am Lucia MacPherson, Pharoah's niece."

He took her hand. She had a good strong grip.

"Now," she continued, "I'm going to see what I can do about cleaning these bruises. Filthy as you are, I should probably take a scrub brush to you, but I presume the pain would be intolerable."

"Scrub away," Slocum said.

But she took a clean towel and dabbed carefully at his cuts and bruises. All the while she complained about his dirtiness, which he thought was a bit unfair. It was hard to find a bathhouse on the Blue Rock Trail and he told her so.

"Yes," she said, scrubbing the cut on his side where George's boot heels had caught him, "I suppose that's true. Did I hurt you? I'm sorry. George Ives is such a despicable little man."

"He ain't no friend of mine."

"So Opal said. She told Uncle that you were down in that hole and would probably die before morning. Uncle is Blue Rock's major employer and he undertook to grant your parole."

When Opal returned with Slocum's new duds, she stood about as close to Lucia MacPherson as she could. Protection.

Lucia was a tall, brisk woman—mid-20s, Slocum guessed—with the kind of poise that could attend a reception for royalty or run a hospital ward filled with wounded soldiers. A very efficient, very aristocratic lady. Her full blouse showed that she was all woman, but most of the woman was restrained, hemmed in.

She had a high forehead, quick blue eyes and a wide, generous mouth. Her hands on John Slocum were deft and gentle.

Surrounded by warmth for the first time in four days, he could hardly keep his eyes open.

"Would you like a little more brandy, Mr. Slocum?" she asked.

"John."

"Very well, then—John." She smiled and handed him another cup of laced tea. Opal stood slightly behind her with the bundle of clothes and a funny kid's grin on her face. "You gonna die on us?" she demanded.

"Nonsense," Lucia MacPherson snapped. "Mr. Slocum is accustomed to much more pain than this. Isn't that correct?"

She was looking at Slocum's scars. He wore a knife cut across his chest. Perez Machado had done a pretty good job on him until he'd got the knife away and buried it in Machado's fat gut. He had a small, puckered bullet wound in his shoulder and wore the wide white stripes of Yuma Penitentiary on his back.

Slocum eyeballed Opal Hevener and liked what he saw: her high young breasts pushing at her bodice; her brown hair plaited down her back. Beside Lucia MacPherson, she looked like a child—a mischievous, tough little street urchin—but she held her body like she knew what it was for, and Slocum was glad the bath water was covering his groin.

She sensed something of his embarrassment and giggled. Lucia gave her an uncomprehending look, and Slocum might have blushed himself if he hadn't been lobster red already.

Now, if these two women were both naked and playful right here in this old bathtub, Slocum thought, *I'd be in heaven sure enough. And I always expected the opposite destination.*

"I understand you refused to fight Mr. Beidler," Lucia said. "I approve of that." Before Slocum could respond, she continued: "I see from your body, however, that you are not unacquainted with violence. While I cannot pretend to understand your change of heart, I certainly commend it."

Which was Slocum's cue to get out of the bath. Slocum wasn't a small man, and right now he was in his full glory. Lucia glanced down, then glanced up. She was rather shocked. *Whatever she approves of,* Slocum thought, a little grimly, *it sure ain't that.*

"Thought you'd seen a lot of stallions," he observed

as the openly staring Opal Hevener handed him a towel as big as a horse blanket.

The rough weave of the towel pulled at Slocum's new cuts and it was like getting cut again. It didn't get any better when Lucia insisted on coating them with iodine. "I don't believe we'll bandage these," Lucia said. "Fresh air will close them up satisfactorily. Mr. Slocum, where is your home?"

Slocum looked at her, surprised. "Yonder," he said.

But the tall, aristocratic woman had the British code of manners: Once you were properly introduced—and somehow Slocum's bath stood for a proper introduction—a well-mannered person inquired about the other's family and estates. "Mr. Slocum, where were you born?"

"Georgia," he said laconically.

"That's a rather large state, Mr. Slocum. Would you care to be somewhat more specific?"

"No, ma'am," Slocum said, "I wouldn't care to be more specific." Once he was dressed, he pulled up a chair and rested his boot heels on the stove.

"I was born in the Cotswolds," Lucia said. "My family has land there and I suppose I've been spoiled all my life." She made the surprising admission in the same tone of voice she would have announced another round of tea. "And Pharoah—"

"Was born in Egypt. Napoleonic wars. Father at the battle of the Nile," Slocum finished her sentence with his guess.

"And Pharoah's wooden leg?"

"Scottish regiment, probably. He lost his leg in India—the Sepoy Mutiny—or in the Crimea."

"Very good. It was the Crimea, actually. He rode with Lord Ragland."

"Well!" Pharoah MacPherson cried from the doorway. "I see you're up and about. Splendid, splendid." He brought some of the outdoors chill in with him on his clothes, and despite himself, Slocum shivered. "Very bracing climate, don't you think?"

Slocum didn't.

"I see you and Lucia've had a chance to get acquainted. Isn't she a marvelous girl?"

"Uncle," Lucia advised sweetly, "go to hell."

"It's true. Temper like a fishwife, of course. Gets her in a bit of trouble, that temper does." He poured himself a generous tot of brandy. "Cheers." As he unwound a long scarlet muffler, he kept talking—as usual, nonstop. "Can't say old Sheriff Hammer was too pleased to be roused up. He wasn't too taken by my description of the night's events, either. He has a foul mouth when he has a mind to use it. 'MacPherson,' he grunts, 'you're in bad trouble.' Oh, releasing *his* prisoner and all that. Threatened to bring me up on charges. So I told him I would personally accompany Mr. Slocum to the next miners' court if and when such an event should be scheduled but, in the meantime, there's no sense letting a man of his talents go to waste." He walked around Slocum like a man inspecting a side of beef. He was rubbing his hands together. "Slocum," he asked suddenly, "do you have any rabbits?"

"Rabbits?"

"Rabbits, partridge—any small game."

"No." From the way MacPherson stared at him, Slocum didn't know if he was supposed to produce rabbits and birds out of his hat.

"Oh, that is a shame. I'd heard you'd sold a splendid elk and I was so hoping you'd have a couple of hares or a brace of partridge in your saddlebags somewhere."

"Just the elk."

"What a pity." He laughed. "Well, what shall we do with you now?" To show he didn't mean anything by his joke, he opened his humidor, selected two Havanas and tossed one to Slocum.

"Much obliged." Slocum lit the cigar, drew deep and was content. With half an ear, he listened while MacPherson rambled on. Apparently MacPherson was the family chef. "Fine cooking," he declared, "is the most delicate and temporal of the arts."

54

"Uh-huh."

Apparently Lucia was a "free spirit." She couldn't boil an egg. While in London, Lucia had been rather too free even for a "free spirit." She'd joined the suffragettes. One afternoon a party of determined young ladies crashed by the Sergeant at Arms into the House of Lords. Inside, they pursued individual Lords through the House with what the *Times* called a list of "impertinent demands." The Lords were appalled. Queen Victoria was, for the record, extremely upset (though Lucia doubted the depth of the old queen's feelings).

The Lords ordered the suffragettes' arrest. Imprisoned at Bow Street, a dank, dirty police station in the heart of one of the grimmer sections of London, the suffragettes announced to the newspapers that they would not eat until they were released, calling their action "a hunger strike."

The newspapers duly reported this, and just two days after they'd begun their strike, the officials reacted. They transported the suffragettes to Charing Cross Hospital, where they force-fed them with tubes down their throats.

Several women died. Lucia's father, an influential man, prevailed upon the authorities for her release. They let her go once they'd extracted a promise from her to leave the country and stay away. As far as possible.

Slocum thought Blue Rock was pretty nearly "as far as possible" and said so.

MacPherson guffawed. Lucia didn't crack a smile.

MacPherson changed the subject. "How much do you know about placer mining, Mr. Slocum?"

Like most drifters, Slocum knew quite a lot. Once he'd had a claim on the Popo Agee that never amounted to much, and another time he'd shared a slightly better claim outside Telluride until somebody back-shot his partner as he was working the sluicebox. When all the smoke had settled, three claim jumpers were lying in the mud beside him—put down by John Slocum's bullets.

Placer mining was a fine way to go broke or get killed. You'd start with gravel or sandbars near the mouth of a good-sized river. You'd pan a couple of panfuls of sand, sloshing it in a circular motion until centrifugal force hurled all the dirt and silica quartz out of the pan, leaving a fine layer of heavier material. Usually it was just black sand: magnetite. Sometimes there were a couple of rough sapphires, but usually they weren't gem quality. Next, you'd hold a magnet over the black sand and uncover the color: the first faint trickles of gold.

Once you found color, you headed upstream, looking for the mother lode. Theory was that the stream, in some previous geological epoch, had cut through a stratum of gold-bearing rock, and all you had to do was stroll up the river and find it.

Of course, it wasn't quite that easy. The Indians didn't love the crazy white men seeking the yellow metal, and more than one prospector's scalp had decorated a Sioux medicine lance. Not to mention claim jumpers. Not to mention road agents.

And, of course, there might not *be* a mother lode. Maybe the entire gold-bearing body had been washed downstream. That's what had happened at Nevada City, though in Deadwood they'd found the mother lode and there were millions of dollars in it, too.

Slocum knew a bit about placer mining and said so.

"Good," MacPherson said. "Then you'll be interested to know that our Britannia, here, is destined to be as famous as the Comstock or the Alice or the Anaconda. The Britannia claims sit on the richest vein of gold anywhere in the country."

"Seems to me I've heard mining men make boasts before," Slocum drawled. "Usually they were lookin' to sell a few shares of stock. Often they were willin' to let me in on the ground floor."

While Slocum spoke, he watched Opal Hevener out

56

of the corner of his eye. That little girl sure was *interested* in him.

MacPherson laughed. "I hardly think Megathorp Mining is interested in promoting a few odd-lot stock sales. Come with me. I have something to show you."

Opal took that as her cue to leave and started buttoning a heavy man's jacket.

"You can't go home now," Lucia exclaimed. "If you return to Blue Rock, the sheriff or that animal George Ives will make you pay dearly for Mr. Slocum's escape."

The girl looked confused. She also looked a little scared.

Lucia decided for her. "You stay here. You can sleep in my room until we find something more suitable, and I shall be happy to offer you employment. I could use some help around this dirty, dusty house."

Pharoah urged Opal to stay. And it didn't really take that much urging.

The two women excused themselves and went off upstairs. Watching them, Slocum couldn't decide which he liked better: the freshness of Opal or the womanly promise of Lucia.

Pharoah escorted Slocum to the back of the house. Bad weather had interrupted the plastering and they'd decided to leave the finish coat until spring. Consequently, the back rooms were dark-brown caves filled with shrouded furniture and packing crates. In what would be the kitchen, a few flimsy wooden chairs lined the walls, and in the center of the floor a large object rested, covered with a green tarpaulin.

"This is why I know the Britannia is on a rich vein," MacPerson exclaimed as he whipped the tarp aside.

It was a rock. A boulder. It stood about four feet high and must have been the same distance in girth. The rock sat on the floor of the cold kitchen like a primitive god half melted down.

When MacPherson moved his lantern closer to the rock, it gleamed. It gleamed like the brass bumper of a locomotive. It gleamed like everything gold Slocum had ever seen. And it wasn't fool's gold, either. Slocum had seen some pretty good-sized chunks of iron pyrites— the downfall of many amateur prospectors—but this boulder was the real thing.

It was pitted, like a meteorite, and rounded, too. It'd been eroded by aeons of rushing water and melted slightly in some ancient geological furnace. A broad chunk of milky quartz bisected it. The quartz band was almost six inches thick. The rest of the rock was, quite simply, the biggest piece of gold Slocum had ever seen.

"What the hell you doin' with that?" he inquired.

"My miners found it in the sandbar directly beneath the Britannia's main shaft. They were sluicing up the last gravel before we sank the shaft. McMurtry and Stone, their names were. There it is, sir: the 'Biggest Gold Nugget in the World.' "

Slocum suppressed a whistle. "How much you figure that chunk of rock is worth?"

"Well, Blue Rock has no scales suitable for weighing something this big in ounces. We hauled it down to the smithy, who constructed a platform beam scale, using cattle weights. One thousand, nine hundred and eighty-five pounds, sir. In one nugget."

"Jesus."

"Discounting for impurities and the quartz band, it comes to roughly thirty thousand ounces. Gold's at sixteen dollars an ounce. It's worth a little more than a hundred thousand quid."

Slocum was surprised at the calm in his own voice: "What's that in greenbacks?"

"Oh, I'd say roughly five hundred thousand. Think of the pressures that forced that seam of quartz through the gold. Think of the countless aeons it took for the whole of this marvelous stone to be fused together."

Slocum was thinking about half a million dollars.

He was remembering a fellow by the name of "Two-for-a-nickel-Johnny." Two-for-a-nickel worked in the assay office in Deadwood. Whenever he'd weigh some miner's poke of gold dust, he'd run his fingers through his greasy hair. Every Friday he'd get a shampoo and haircut and stand right there while they panned the gold out of his clippings. It was worth an extra $50 a week to him.

"And, of course, it's theft-proof." MacPherson was still chattering. "It's too damn heavy for one man to move. It isn't the sort of thing a sneak thief can stick in his pocket."

Slocum thought he'd sure like to give it a try.

"I've written the home office to apprise them of the discovery. I wrote in September, but the mails being what they are, I haven't had any reply as yet. I could smash it in our stamp mill and send it out with the regular gold trains in the spring, but I'd rather see it intact—one of a kind. Like myself, eh, Slocum?" He laughed.

"Yeah, sure. What happens if some joker decides to come up here one night with a rock hammer and bash himself off a grubstake?"

MacPherson got huffy. "I am familiar with weapons, sir. I own an excellent pair of Colt revolvers and I'd use them, I daresay. Let's return to the front of the house. It's awfully chilly back here."

Slocum was thinking. He was thinking about sleds and rollers and prybars and half a million dollars. Hell, he could retire on that and spend the rest of his days lying around, enjoying the good life, with 20 girls and a couple of hundred horses to keep him company.

MacPherson was still talking about mining. He thought the Britannia was sitting right on a mother lode. He wondered if, once they'd exhausted the gold, they'd hit silver, as they did at the Comstock. "If the Britannia follows a similar geology, five years from now I shall be a very wealthy man."

"If you was to put that rock on a sled and get it to Denver, you could be a very rich man by spring," Slocum said.

"Hah, hah, very funny. You Yanks have such a marvelous sense of humor."

Slocum didn't feel like disillusioning the man. No sense in it.

Outside, the snow was falling again. If Slocum was still in the log dugout, he'd be stiff by now, but Slocum didn't dwell on it. He'd squeaked through too many times. Hell, by all logic, he should have been dead years ago.

So they sat and talked and lowered the level of MacPherson's brandy. They discovered a common interest in military matters and the brand-new invention: the Gatling gun. MacPherson thought it'd never face a full cavalry charge. Slocum thought the horsemen would be shot to ribbons.

MacPherson filled him in on the road agents. With only one road out of Blue Rock, they pretty much had a free rein. They never made big hauls—just two or three victims at a time. MacPherson's gold trains were safe because he didn't separate the gold from the pulverized ore until a week before the trains left for Fort Bozeman. He laughed: "Too heavy. Too much trouble. We've had no holdup attempts at the mine, because what thief would steal a hundred pounds of pulverized rock in order to get one pound of gold?"

Pretty shrewd. Slocum knew a few thieves who might have tried it, but they were thief artists who couldn't resist a difficult challenge. Slocum didn't say anything about them. He merely remarked, "anything valuable one man has, another man's gonna think up some way of stealin' it."

MacPherson grinned. "You know, Slocum, I've a funny feeling about you. I'm rather pleased I got you out of that damn frozen hole. I wouldn't want to have you thinking hard about the Britannia's gold."

Quite seriously Slocum replied, "No, you wouldn't."

And they sipped their brandy in a companionable silence broken only by the crackling of the fire in the cast-iron stove.

Megathorp Mining had picked a pretty good manager for their western operations. MacPherson wasn't the
first Englishman Slocum had met out west. Hell, English
investors owned half the cattle ranches and three quar-
ters of the mines west of the Mississippi. But too many
of them made no attempt to understand the wild country or the wild men who were taming it. Ignorance in
wild country was too often fatal. MacPherson was an
unusually smart man, and Slocum warmed to him.

The mantel clock struck. MacPherson yawned and
stretched. "I have an early morning of it tomorrow,"
he announced. "Perhaps you could reclaim your rifles
and scout up some game. I'll pay top prices for elk."

Slocum spread out blankets on the chaise, got under
them, and slipped a velveteen pillow under his head.

The house creaked in the wind and the stove
popped as the pine knots exploded in the firebox, and
for just a moment before he fell asleep, John Slocum
thought that he'd been lucky all his life. He wondered
if whoever had given him all that luck had some plans
for him.

He woke suddenly. His hand slipped under his
pillow. No Colt. He opened one eye slowly.

"You're so darn slick, John Slocum," Opal Hevener
said. "Maybe too slick for your own good."

"Thought that a time or two myself." Slocum's voice
was gentle, with just a hint of a drawl. He'd been an
outlaw, a hard man. He'd been quick to take offense
and quicker to act on it, but Slocum had also been
born and raised in a household where men were not
the less men for being gentle.

Opal crouched beside his bed on her haunches. She
was wearing a flannel robe fastened up to her throat.
The robe was too long for her; Slocum guessed it had
come from one of Lucia MacPherson's trunks.

"Get in here, girl," he said, "before you catch your
death of cold."

She shrugged out of her robe and stood proudly
before him.

61

The moonlight shone off the snow and washed the inside of the room with gentle white light. Her breasts were small but full—a girl's breasts. Slocum could have encircled her waist with his two hands. Below, the slow flare of her hips and the warm triangle she was offering him. He looked at her for a long time because that's what she wanted; it was going to be a slow pleasure.

Her body slipped in beside him, warm and sleek as a baby seal. He could feel her heart beat against his chest, and her hair fanned across his face and tickled him. She cuddled in his arms and carefully, deliberately, her tongue kissed and licked at his eyes, her tongue darting like a hummingbird.

Her hand slipped to his groin and found him. "My god, John Slocum," she whispered, "how the dickens is that thing gonna fit? I ain't no twelve-gauge, you know. I'm only a four-ten." She giggled softly, but her hand was real interested in him and she was kissing his ear.

He ran his hands behind her small ass and stroked her and reached between her legs and touched her center. She gasped a little at his touch, but she was ready.

He lifted her by her hips and slipped himself in, just a little. When he scratched her back gently, she settled on him a bit. She was small, all right, but Slocum wasn't in any great hurry and he stroked her and they kissed, exploring each other, and she eased down onto him a half-inch at a time. Her breasts were nubbins hard against his chest and she rolled them against his chest hair, stretching herself like a cat. Her belly touched his like a feather. Her hips lurched and she sat straight up and closed her eyes and she rode him down.

She said, "Goddamn, John, you're a good old boy," and she was bucking then like a horse he'd ridden to a standstill in Wyoming last summer—a crazy white horse with one red eye that Slocum had approached real slow, the horse backing away from him, and Slocum throwing his cigarette butt in the dust. He'd bet

$50 he could ride that horse, and the other punchers were hanging on the corral rail, yelling, slapping their hats against their legs, making as much damn racket as they could, so that the killer horse was half out of its mind with fear before Slocum whipped the bit into its mouth and threw his leg over its back. The horse broke bad, crawfishing and bucking on rigid steel legs, and Slocum almost lost it the first time his groin hit that knobby white back. He jerked back on the bit to straighten the mare out and it went back on its hocks and slid, in a tremendous cloud of dust, and the cowboys were hollering, thinking the 50 bucks was as good as in their pocket, but when the dust settled and the mare was up again, Slocum was stuck tight to its back like a burr.

That horse jumped up and down, regular as a pump handle. Every now and again it varied the stroke—stayed down deeper and then exploded. When the mare had been at it for ten minutes, Slocum leaned forward along its sleek, elongated neck, put his teeth to its ear and seized it.

Opal was moaning and her small hips were working and he clamped her butt fast, pulled her to him and held her there while she cried out and contracted round him.

After she dismounted, she curled around him like a child. She butted him with her head so he'd make a little more room on the narrow chaise.

"Slocum," she whispered, "thanks."

"Sure."

She nuzzled him with her nose and giggled and he gave her a smack on the butt and she said, "You want to start somethin', mister, you better be sure you can finish it."

In the darkness, Slocum smiled.

She traced his smile with her fingertips. "Slocum," she said softly, "I'm scared."

"George?"

"Uh-huh. Him and Sheriff Hammer both. They ain't

gonna be none too happy about this—you gettin' out and all."

"Everybody's scared of something," Slocum said.

"But Georgie . . . he . . ."

"I don't think Georgie's gonna be botherin' anybody until he heals. Maybe I'll just make sure he stays sick."

"Slocum, what are you scared of?" She was breathing softly against his neck, her sweat-slick skin drying next to his.

"Myself. Only thing I ever thought was worrisome enough."

"John, you ever been married?"

"No."

"Why ever not?"

"If I ever got married, I wouldn't have little hillbilly girls slippin' into my bed at night."

"Here's one little hillbilly girl that kind of likes slippin' into your bed at night."

When they made love again, it was slower, quieter, their first need spent. They went deep. They explored each other's secrets. At the end, it was hard for Slocum to tell where she stopped and he started. They were, simply, together.

Outside, the wind was peeling the new snow off the bare blue ice and sending it spinning like some soft abrasive against the walls.

Inside, there was only the pop of the stove and the hush of their breathing.

4

She'd slipped away before Slocum awoke, leaving only a faint fragrance behind her.

Lucia MacPherson was stomping around the stove, attacking the skillets and bowls like they were personal enemies. She was breaking eggs into a stoneware bowl like she wished she was breaking something else, and Slocum had a pretty good idea what that something else might be. But the dazzling sun was spreading a warm pattern across the green and yellow rug, and John Slocum stretched and yawned and, naked, jumped out of bed.

"Mornin'," he said. He stared at the eggs running together in a pan and sniffed. "Hope nobody ever tells the chicken about this."

"Mr. Slocum, are you accustomed to lounging around in the morning without a stitch? Others may be impressed by your manly physique, but I've seen others and better."

"Yes'm," Slocum said. "So you said last night." He scratched his ass. He slipped into red flannels and a pair of cavalry twills. He drew on heavy packer's boots over wool socks and took a pitcher of water outside to rinse his face. The air was dead clear, it was cold, and a wan sun was doing its best but wasn't enough to warm his bones. The water was icy on his face but brought him all the way awake in a hurry.

When he went back into the kitchen, he pulled on a wool checked shirt and stretched again. His muscles were a little sore, but exercise would soon work the stiffness out of them.

"Coffee, Mr. Slocum?"

He took it as a truce declaration and said sure, thanks, even though she insisted on calling him by that damn "Mister" and just couldn't let go of it.

The coffee was as bitter and mean as a miser's disposition, but he figured it wasn't intentional; she just didn't know better.

He watched her work over the stove and thought she hadn't had a whole lot of practice. Her hands flew everywhere, but she couldn't ever find exactly what she was looking for. She dropped the stove-plate lifter at least three times, and once she had to go down on her hands and knees to retrieve it. Slocum rolled himself a smoke.

She was a fine figure of a woman: long fingers, long legs and the ripeness of a woman grown. But Slocum thought she wasn't as practiced as she made out to be.

With a clatter, she set the plate in front of him and the scrambled eggs almost slid off. He took her wrist and said quietly, "Lucia, if you want to throw them at me, just throw them. Don't go pretending it was accidental."

She flushed to the roots of her hair. "You're so god-damned smart," she snapped.

He grinned at her and stabbed his fork into the rubbery yellow mess. The bacon was burnt and the eggs were overdone and way too salty, but he'd eaten worse and he was hungry enough for three bronc jumpers at a jamboree.

She didn't eat with him. She sat across the table and stared at the steady movement of his jaws.

"You ain't hungry?" he asked finally.

"No. I just take a little tea and biscuits at ten."

He inspected her long, angular frame. "No wonder you ain't got no meat on you," he said.

"You are a bit of a bastard, Mr. Slocum."

"Name's John."

"John the seducer?"

He set down his fork and pushed the plate away from him. "Now, what would you be knowing about se-duction?" He grinned at her.

She was beet red, and her hands were clenched so hard her knuckles showed white. "She's just a child," she snapped.

Now he understood. Opal was sleeping in Lucia's room last night. Probably Lucia awoke when Opal slipped out and waited there, sleepless, until she crept back in at dawn. Maybe she tried not to listen for noises downstairs and maybe she did listen, all ears.

"Didn't seem like any child to me," he said. He built a couple of smokes to take with him and drained the last bitter dregs of his coffee.

But she wasn't quite ready to let it go. "You're a fine one, taking advantage of a young, trusting girl."

Slocum rose, set his hat at a nice angle and opened

the door before he said, "You mean next time I should wait until the *woman* of the house comes down the stairs?" And he had the door closed behind him when the skillet whanged into it. John Slocum laughed and it felt real good. He thought, *By God, this is going to be a hell of a day.*

He wasn't far wrong.

As he strolled down the middle of Blue Rock's main street, he felt eyes on him. Passing miners broke their conversations and stared after his back. The storekeeper found some excuse to linger outside his door. The two Indian whores from Walker's leaned out the window and one yelled, "Hey, cowboy! How 'bout comin' upstairs and givin' me a tumble?"

Slocum gave the blowsy woman a cheerful wave.

He turned into the darkness of the livery stable. The stable was three attached log rooms, with a hayloft under the low roof and new oak grain bins lining the walkway between the stalls. A neat operation: the harnesses and saddles hung on pegs, the grain buckets neatly stacked in the corner. Slocum was glad to find somebody had brushed down and blanketed his Appaloosa. It was chewing contentedly on a bucket of rolled corn.

"Some says give 'em oats," a voice said. "But I say, in this high country in the winter, they won't founder on good corn nohow."

The speaker was a little black man, not much larger than a jockey, and from the way his legs were bowed, maybe he'd been one once. He wore a full-length leather apron and a neat black bowler hat.

"You the liveryman?" Slocum asked.

"I ain't the liveryman's nigger," the black man replied. Maybe he was reacting to Slocum's question, but most likely he was reacting to Slocum's Southern drawl.

"I suppose you're one of those uppity niggers," Slocum said softly.

"I sure as hell am."

"You run a good operation here," Slocum said. "I ain't seen a cleaner livery since I left Denver."

The praise was meant and the black man knew it and his face lit up in a grin. "North Carolina?" he guessed.

"Nope. Georgia. You?"

"Blue-grass country. Kentucky."

"Nice country that."

"Yep. After the war, there wasn't anything for us in Kentucky, so me and my wife we decided to come north and find that city they was tellin' us about, the one with the streets of gold."

"Yeah." Slocum rubbed his Appaloosa, which nickered to return the compliment. "I been lookin' for that same damn city seems like most of my life."

"Any luck?"

"Nope. You?"

"I'm standin' on the street."

"Looks more like horseshit than gold to me." Slocum laughed.

"Least I'm free," the black man came right back at him.

"Yeah. I know." And Slocum did, too. "What do I owe you for takin' such good care of my horses?"

A funny, frightened look flashed across the black man's face. "Nothin'," he said nervously. "I don't want nothin'."

Slocum had his poke in his hand—a loan from Pharoah MacPherson—ready to pinch out a couple of dollars' worth of gold dust. "I don't like for a man to work for me without gettin' paid," he said.

"No." The black man was insisting too much, and Slocum began to feel a crawling along his spine, like maybe a rifle was zeroed on him.

"No," the black man said. "I'm sorry, but I ain't gonna rob no graves. I don't want no dead man's money."

Slocum pocketed his pouch. "So old Georgie's been around."

The black man nodded. He didn't like being scared, but he was, clean through.

"Okay. Why don't you go ahead and saddle up that bay gelding packhorse of mine while I go see Georgie and straighten him out? I aim to do a little huntin' this afternoon and I wouldn't want to be thinkin' about Georgie when I should be concentratin' on elk."

When he strolled out, the liveryman was glad to see him go.

By now the news of Slocum's presence had spread. Bored miners leaned against the store fronts and peered out of the low windows of their dugouts as he ambled down the street.

Everybody's real interested in my business, Slocum thought, without amusement.

Jim Thiel stepped out in front of him. Thiel put both his hands out as though he was warding something off, or maybe he was just showing he didn't have a gun. "Slocum."

"Mornin', Thiel. You happen to know where I can pick up my belongings?"

"Your horses—they're at the livery."

"The guns."

Thiel's face was lined with concern. "All your stuff is still down at Walker's Saloon," he said. "But if I was you, I'd leave 'em stay right there. I'd get on my horse and ride the hell out of Blue Rock."

Slocum's eyes flared up suddenly, and Thiel, looking at them, was real glad he wasn't John Slocum's enemy. "Yeah." Slocum spoke softly. "I'm a market hunter, Thiel. How the hell am I gonna hunt game without my rifles?"

Thiel was sweating, but he was obliged to deliver his warning. "Slocum, they're waitin' for you in there. You ain't comin' out again unless it's feet first."

Slocum glanced around, took a deep breath of clear mountain air and smiled. "Well, Thiel, thanks for the warnin'. But ain't it a great day to die?"

A couple of watchers slipped into Walker's when

Slocum put his boots on the boardwalk outside. A respectable crowd of miners was behind him.

Slocum leaned against the outside of the saloon, pulled out one of his smokes, struck a match on the doorframe and fired up. He watched the men watching him, through a cloud of tobacco. The men in the first rank got real nervous and looked in every direction but his.

Slocum knew his tools. He was lucky—he knew that —but he had another big advantage in a fight. More than once, when the odds were stacked against him, he'd come out alive when other men were pushing up daisies. Slocum stood in the morning sunshine, reviewing his life and deciding that it didn't make a damn bit of difference if he was alive or dead.

He worked on his temper a little, letting it come, letting it fill him with icy rage. And the softness went out of his cheeks and whatever gentleness John Slocum knew drained out of him. He looked a little bit like a Cooper's Hawk half crazy from being on the perch too long.

He knew he was making them wait. Fine. It'd throw them off their timing.

He set his mind against guns. He told his hands to reach for flesh, told his eyes not to notice where he could grab for the iron frame of a Colt. He was going to settle this hand to hand.

When he pushed through the saloon doors, every eye turned to him and no eye lingered. His guns were on the near end of the bar. Sheriff Hammer was leaning against the bar halfway down, and little Georgie, his face bandaged up, was standing at the other end, his hand hanging carelessly over his holster. Slocum kept his hands away from his sides. He didn't want them to claim he tried to draw.

"Sheriff Hammer!" he yelled. And the sheriff, who'd been studying his whiskey glass, started and flushed, and George's hand touched his gun butt and a ripple of laughter filled the room from the watching miners.

"How you all doin'?" Slocum inquired genially.

The sheriff shot him a glower. George eased his hand off his Colt. "I suppose you heard MacPherson turned me loose last night," Slocum said. "MacPherson figured you need meat in this town more'n you need a cooked-up story about me bein' a road agent. How does that sit with you?"

Another chuckle from the miners. Somebody said, "That's okay, Slocum. You left a replacement for yourself down in the hoosegow." A few other men laughed, though the sheriff was swiveling his threatening gaze over the crowd like a Prussian gunner sighting cannon.

Good. Slocum had wanted the miners on his side. These men could be, by turns, sentimental to the point of mawkishness, brutal, brave. But give them half a chance and they'd see the truth of the matter. They were like the Indians Slocum had lived with: Courage won their hearts in a minute.

The sheriff turned to face Slocum head on. Sheriff Hammer was a man who looked like he'd never tasted the bitterness of defeat, never had his pride trampled in the dust. "You got no right," he blustered. "You're an escaped prisoner—from the Blue Rock jail, by God."

"Sheriff, don't be a jackass. Your face gets all swelled up when you get mad. You got nothin' to worry about. I'm on parole to Mr. MacPherson, and any time you want to hold another miners' court, I'll be there." He turned to the crowd. "He got any reason to worry about me skippin' town?" he asked.

One young miner grinned. "Hell no." A couple of the other miners said "Hell no" and "MacPherson's word is good."

Slocum slapped Hammer on the shoulder, "So you see, pal," he said, "you got nothin' to worry about. Where's your buddy Beidler?"

"He's . . . he's out scouting around the town."

"Well, good for him." Slocum leaned over to whisper

confidentially in the sheriff's ear, "I wouldn't trust that Kraut bastard if I was you. He ain't a very nice man."

Slocum brushed by the sheriff. Hammer was helpless now. He wouldn't try anything with a Slocum-friendly crowd watching his every move.

Now it was between Slocum and Georgie.

Georgie didn't look too good. He was a little white around the gills and his right hand was trembling. Slocum kept coming until ten feet separated them. He turned and leaned on the bar. "Walker," he called, "how about a shot down here, or ain't you runnin' a saloon no more?"

Walker bustled over with a bottle and tried to leave very quick. He said, "On the house. On the house."

Slocum caught his wrist in a steel grip and said, "Naw, Walker. Hell, you bought me one last night when you didn't know me from Adam and I sure didn't look to be no regular customer." He released Walker's wrist to pinch out some dust. "Have one with me, Walker," he urged. "And bring one down to George there. We got a lot in common, him and me, and I'd hate to see him standin' there without a drink in his hand."

Walker poured the drinks with a shaking hand and slid George's down the bar. He drank nervously. The booze he slopped out of his glass ran down his chin.

Slocum ambled down the bar another five feet, his drink in his right hand and his left hand well clear of his side. George's fingers were jumping around like he had St. Vitus's dance, and he hadn't touched his drink.

"What's the matter, Georgie?" Slocum asked. "You sign the pledge? You off the stuff?"

Slocum heard a foot scuffle behind him, but it was just some nervous miner getting out of the line of fire.

"You ever know Luke Short?" Slocum asked conversationally. " 'Black Powder' Luke Short. Gambler. Pretty good at stud or draw, just a fair hand at red dog and faro. Texican."

If George knew Luke Short, he didn't care to talk about him.

"Well, Luke Short isn't fast, not fast at all. He's a gutsy bastard, though. He gets in real close to his man —oh, no farther'n I am from you—and he wears one of those .41 double derringers in a sleeve clip. He ain't much of a shot. But if Short misses with the first barrel, the muzzle blast just naturally sets the other man's clothes on fire, and while he's beatin' at himself, tryin' to put it out, old Luke's got all the time in the world. All the time in the world."

George was wondering if Slocum carried a derringer. His face was crinkled up with worry. He was beginning to think he'd made a bad mistake.

Carefully Slocum unbuttoned his left shirt cuff. Very slowly he rolled it back. Every eye in the place was on Slocum's right hand, expecting it to flash for a hidden derringer.

And he kicked George Ives in the balls.

George rode the foot up in the air, his eyes bulging out of his head and a great whoosh of air rushing out of his lungs.

George's eye had seen some blur of Slocum's boot and he'd grabbed for his Colt. He had it half out when Slocum connected and the pistol passed through his hands like it was trivial and didn't matter a bit. It landed somewhere behind him. George was in so much pain he didn't care. He landed heavily on his butt and had just an instant to see Slocum's other boot before it connected with the side of his head and he blacked out.

Slocum picked up George's unfinished drink and drained it. "No sense lettin' good whiskey go to waste," he observed.

He bent and rummaged through George's pockets until he found his money. Carefully Slocum extracted one double eagle. He faced the crowd. He smiled. Slocum had the eyes of a wolf. "I'm a peaceable man," he announced. "But this man stole twenty dollars out of my pocket and I ain't no public charity."

One of the miners laughed and pretty soon the whole place was laughing.

Slocum tossed the double eagle to the bartender. It winked as it spun through the light. "Walker, you take this money," Slocum said, "and you set 'em up for these boys until it's all gone. I don't want to hang onto it any longer. It's been keepin' bad company."

A cheer from the miners and suddenly everybody wanted to shake Slocum's hand, but he didn't care for that foolishness, so he slipped out as soon as he gracefully could. With all his guns.

He stopped at the general store just long enough to buy a pair of Indian snowshoes. They'd been sitting in the storeroom since God knows when, but the rawhide webbing wasn't dried out and the good mountain ash hadn't sprung. Slocum gave the last of his gold dust for them. He lugged all his gear over to the livery.

"Didn't expect to see you again," the black man remarked.

"Yeah, well I wasn't too sure I'd be back myself, tell the truth," Slocum said.

And they laughed together. The black man had saddled his bay gelding packhorse and, yes, there was a sled in the tackroom Slocum could borrow.

"I'll bring you some prime meat," Slocum said. "Much obliged."

He left his shotguns with the liveryman and lashed the Sharps, the Winchester and the Colt revolving rifle on the packhorse's back. The horse had drawn a buggy before, and Slocum didn't expect it'd have trouble pulling the wide-bottomed sled.

For a few miles down the Blue Rock Trail, Slocum led the horse. The sky was clear, the sun at this altitude hot enough to burn the skin. Slocum kept a wary eye for avalanche tracks.

Above him, above the timberline, the snow and ice had collected all winter, alternately freezing and thawing. In some places only a fragile bond of ice kept hundreds of tons of snow from sliding down the mountainside. As the sun warmed the ice and it pulled away from the rock, the bond would weaken and the slightest noise could shatter the fragile glue and send a mass of snow, ice, boulders and broken trees roaring down the slope.

Twice he stopped to listen to the distant boom as an avalanche exploded somewhere deeper in the mountains. In this clear mountain air, the sound of a slide could travel for five or ten miles. Slocum didn't worry about the distant slides, but he wasn't real enthused about anything much closer.

Once he had to cross an old avalanche track—a jumble of debris and boulders across the trail. He led his horse very carefully, winding around the broken boulders and tree trunks. He was clucking softly to the horse. New avalanches followed old avalanche tracks as regular as express trains, so Slocum clucked softly and walked softly, too. Slides had been started by a shout or a rifle shot—sometimes it didn't take much—and the snow cliffs towering above him and his tiny horse didn't fill him with confidence. Every clink of the horse's harness made him wince; and once, when the sled was wedged between two boulders, he freed it careful as a surgeon.

After the track, he made better time, and the sun felt warmer on his back. When a wide glacial valley opened up beside the trail, he entered it. The horse found fair footing so long as it kept to the windward slope, though the snow was quite deep in the bottom.

Gradually the valley broadened. The timber was sparse and blown into tortured shapes by the wind.

The old mountain men used to winter in sheltered valleys like this one from October until May. Easier if you were alone. If two men holed up together, they'd likely have killed each other or be buggering each other by ice out.

Slocum was looking for elk, but he wouldn't pass up a deer or a bighorn or mountain goat. He didn't have much hope of a goat. The only men who killed the funny-looking, agile Rocky Mountain goats were European sportsmen, with their elaborate rifles, guides, camp cooks and all the time in the world to clamber around the narrow, dangerous ledges the goats called home.

Slocum didn't much want a goat, anyway. He was a meat hunter, not a trophy hunter, and hardly anybody liked to eat goat unless they couldn't get anything else.

About halfway up the valley he had a piece of luck, but he couldn't make anything out of it. Above him, on the right, he spotted four bighorn sheep. They were fat and sassy and way the hell out of reach. Slocum shaded his eyes. The sheep were perhaps 1,500 yards away. He took a sea captain's telescope out of his pack and looked them over: pretty fine animals. The lead was a big doe, followed by a stocky, older buck with the heavy curled horns that looked like seashells curled around. Stepping carefully in the buck's tracks were two yearlings: a spike buck and another smallish doe. The yearlings would be good eating. The fat was no good and the meat was a mite gamy, but they'd fetch a good price in Blue Rock.

Slocum adjusted the sights on his Sharps .69. The sheep had probably spotted him, but he was far away and this was their country and they weren't giving him a thought.

He leaned the Sharps against a stubby jack pine and drew a careful bead on the trailing yearling. Once more, before he fired, he checked the herd with his telescope and it was no good. No good at all. He could kill the bighorn, all right, but the body would fall a couple of hundred feet to a broad ledge where it'd lie until Slocum made the laborious climb up to it, or until, more likely, some grizzly found it in the spring.

Slocum was no Alpinist. Some men in Europe, he'd heard, had started climbing the tallest mountains for the thrill of it. Slocum had plenty of danger in his daily life without going after more.

Regretfully, he slipped the Sharps back into its Indian scabbard and watched the sheep until they were out of sight. Beautiful damn critters, walking easily where no man could. He didn't regret not getting a shot.

Before the morning was out, he let another animal go. When the snow finally got too deep for his pack-horse, he tethered it, strapped the snowshoes to his feet and continued up the narrowing valley. He left the Sharps and the Winchester with the horse, though he knew he was a damn fool for carrying the Colt.

The Colt revolving rifle was designed like the Colt single-action revolver. The revolver, in the hands of an expert, was accurate to 150 yards. The revolving rifle added just 50 yards to that. It was a lot more fragile than the Winchester and not half as accurate. Slocum didn't even like the caliber—.38-.50. A fine caliber for a lady's hideout pistol but too light for a serious hunter.

Slocum carried the Colt revolving rifle because the action was identical to that of the short guns he'd sworn not to carry, and he didn't want to entirely lose his touch. He felt like a damn fool.

The second animal Slocum passed up was a cow buffalo. His snowshoes were practically silent; he came at it from above—above its scent line—and it didn't have much of a chance to get spooked. The cow'd wallowed down in a copse of pines; Slocum caught a flicker of movement, and silent as a ghost, he slipped down to check it out.

Damn ugly thing. Heavy head and hump, and it was bred, too. Slocum could see the swelling on its sides, though how it had got bred with buffalo as scarce as they were was some kind of tribute either to the species or to the cow's own stubborn determination.

Once, in 1870, Slocum saw a herd of buffalo that took two days to pass. The wagon train he was escort-ing waited in a dust cloud so thick it filtered the bright yellow sunlight into a gray haze while the bawling beasts passed on their annual migration from Canada to Texas. The hide hunters had killed them all. Buffalo had got so scarce Slocum hadn't seen but two this year, and this old pregnant cow made the third.

The cow still hadn't spotted him, though he wasn't more than 50 yards from it. It was busy stripping bark from some fir trees. Maybe it'd make it through the winter. Slocum watched and listened to the animal chew the fibrous bark and said, "Hell. You're tough as boot leather. You ain't worth the trouble to butcher."

The cow looked up, surprised at the interruption, and then got real alarmed and lowered its head, and for a moment Slocum thought he was going to have to kill it anyway. He backed upslope, talking softly to the animal: "Easy, girl. No sense gettin' yourself killed. Besides, you got a calf inside you and you'd lose it, too."

Maybe the cow understood. Maybe it didn't have the energy for an uphill charge. It stopped pawing the ground, glared at Slocum and went back to its feeding before he was amid the pines again and lost to its sight.

Slocum saw plenty of small animal tracks. The jack-rabbits were the most common: broad, splayfooted tracks with the drag track between. He noted the tiny tracks of a marten—hunting the same jacks—and the catlike marks of a mink beside the icy creek that centered the valley. He passed a couple of abandoned beaver lodges. To support John Jacob Astor and the craze for genuine beaver hats, the trappers had come this far and trapped the beaver out, every one.

There's no part of this country that hasn't seen white men now, Slocum thought, and the thought made him sad.

Slocum was hunting elk: the beef of the high Rockies. The meat was sweet, and a good animal would yield 300 pounds of it. They'd be up here, too, in some dense alder or cottonwood thicket, near enough to water, protected from the weather.

When most men saw a big buck elk with its does, they thought of a sultan in a harem: absolute ruler of his band of females and children. Slocum thought that was pretty funny. The old does led the herd, faced danger first, and the big impressive buck? It was their pet. Slocum'd spent a few hours watching wild animals. The does pampered and caressed their buck, but they made all the important decisions.

Maybe man's the only animal where women don't do all the work. Slocum grinned.

The ground was looking more likely now. As it neared the headwall, the valley was breaking up. Towering cliffs protected the trees from the prevailing winds, and the trees were larger and straighter. The underbrush was dense, and Slocum had to watch his footing.

Slocum's breath was freezing on his muffler. His pant legs were frozen to his ankles. He kept the Colt rifle loose in his arms, ready in case a meat animal burst out of the heavy timber.

When he stepped into the clearing, he knew something was real wrong.

The clearing wasn't more than 50 feet across, entirely surrounded by big Douglas firs with the sheer wall of the rimrock rising behind them. An ancient avalanche had cleared this space, and five feet under the snow was a mess of debris, but the surface was quite smooth and unmarked.

Maybe Slocum smelled him, smelled some faint aroma of woodsmoke and bear grease. Maybe Slocum smelled his sweat.

Slocum was three steps into the clearing, his eyes fixed on the trees ahead of him. He didn't see anything move, but he felt the eyes on him and—bear grease? Woodsmoke?

Though Slocum's heart was slamming messages to his brain, he kept on going, and nobody watching him would have guessed his suspicion or his wary eyes under the slouch hat shading his face.

Suddenly he flipped forward and rolled into the pines on his left.

No shot. No motion.

Slocum hadn't stopped moving once he got into cover. His rifle poked out in front of him, he dashed, hunched over another 20 feet and froze, dead still, waiting. He'd got snow in his coat cuffs, and it was starting to melt along his wrists. Thumb on the Colt hammer, John Slocum waited.

He'd startled some magpies with his sudden move. They circled over the pines for a long time before deciding it was safe to land again.

Slocum hunkered in the snow and got colder and colder. His coat was half covered with snow, and his brown hat had clumps of snow stuck to its brim. His feet were cold, his hands were cold, every motionless part of him was cold. He didn't notice. Slocum didn't blink his eyes. Except for the tiny cloud of frost from his breathing, he could have been a statue. He listened. Nothing unusual. He let his nose work, but because the sense of smell is our weakest sense and fades the fastest, he couldn't smell what had first alerted him.

He heard the magpies jumping around in the snow-laden branches.

He heard the wind rustling through the tops of the pines.

He heard the distant thunder of an avalanche—20 miles away, if he was any judge.

Even when he saw the movement, he stayed still. Men have been known to create false movements, and Slocum never shot what he couldn't identify.

Near the bottom of an evergreen, a branch dropped its load of snow with a soft whoosh. The branch waved back and forth like a flag. Slocum didn't stare. He kept his eyes flickering from side to side. Peripheral vision picks up more than staring direct.

He waited half an hour, knees in the snow, rifle ready in his hands, before he spotted the Indian. Even then he didn't move until the brave stepped out of concealment, empty-handed, with one palm raised in the old sign of peaceable intentions.

Slocum let his eyes run over the forest for one last

check before he stood upright, Colt pointed at the sky.

The Indian had good reason to be cautious. Nine out of ten white men would have gunned a single Indian on sight, particularly one who looked this miserable.

From his leggings, he was a Piegan Blackfoot, obviously a little down on his luck, because he was far south of the hunting grounds the Blackfeet claimed. His wolf-fur robe was ratty and patched with cowhide at the elbows. His leggings were black with grease. His rabbit-fur hat looked fairly new, but his face was thin and pale under it. His left arm seemed frozen and swung stiff as a stick at his side. Slocum guessed he was in his mid-20s.

Slocum walked slowly forward. He didn't think this brave had any friends, but it never paid a man to be careless.

Ceremoniously, they walked toward each other, and the brave never took his eyes off the tip of Slocum's rifle. When they were ten feet apart, the buck stopped and Slocum did likewise. Slocum searched the Indian's face. The Indian had obviously been doing some serious starving and his body had burned off most of the fatty deposits just staying alive. Maybe that's what Slocum had smelled: the faint sweet stink of a body feeding on itself—the stink of starvation.

The Indian signed for tobacco. With his left hand, Slocum tossed him the makings. While the Indian built his smoke, Slocum's eyes never stopped searching the undergrowth at the edge of the clearing.

Indians were all language purists, insisting on their own tribal dialects. The Piegan Blackfoot could hardly carry on a conversation with a Blood Blackfoot, let alone with a Shoshoni or a Nez Percé. He relied on the universally understood sign language to communicate with any stranger—anyone outside the tribe.

The Indian had trouble rolling his smoke. His left arm was practically useless, like it'd been broken and mended bad. When he had the smoke going, he was about to toss the tobacco back, but Slocum signed he should keep it. The Indian smiled. It was the first time his face had expressed anything but wariness. He signed his thanks.

It wasn't just tobacco he wanted. As he smoked, his agile brown fingers told their story. Too common, perhaps, but real enough:

He was called Chewaumegan—the "White Beaver." He, his old wife, his young wife and their daughter had been camped a few hours from here. They'd been part of a Piegan band that'd been caught slipping into Canada by the "Long Knives" and the "Redcoats"—the U.S. Cavalry and the Mounties. It wasn't an engagement likely to find a place in the history books.

Near Two Medicine Lake, the Mounties had refused them entry into Canada, and the Long Knives were coming up hard behind them. The Indians had to fight, all 20 of them, but their old hunting bows hadn't been much use against the soldiers' trapdoor Springfields. Chewaumegan and his family had escaped and watched most of the carnage from a nearby ridge. His young wife had cried after seeing her parents cut down, but Chewaumegan had rebuked her tears, saying, "It is what the white men do. Do we complain when the bear-that-walks-like-a-man kills a child? Do we weep when the snow swallows the game?"

But her tears wouldn't stop, and today she sat in their cabin and had no milk to nurse their infant daughter. The old wife did what she could: put out the jackrabbit snares; made a sling to take low-roosting partridges out of the trees. It was not enough. So Chewaumegan had uncased his old war bow, said his good-bys and set out after the elk. He'd found them. If Slocum wished, he'd guide him to a big herd of many, many animals, all fat and healthy. In exchange, he wanted the entrails of the animals Slocum killed. (He knew that white men ate only part of the game.) He touched his bad arm like it was disgusting. It was no longer strong enough to pull the war bow, and without meat, he would sing his death song.

82

As he told his story, his face showed no particular emotion. If Slocum wanted to hunt alone—why, so it would be. Chewaumegan would find a high, barren ridge, remove his tattered wolfskin coat and sing until his breath failed.

Slocum signed, "Where are the elk?"

Still expressionless, the Indian signaled for Slocum to follow.

They slipped around the head of the valley, well above the scent line. The only sound was the occasional crunch of Slocum's snowshoes on the crusted snow.

For a man who was half starved, the Indian moved well. Slocum thought he was running on pure nerve and once that failed, that'd be the end of him.

The elk yard was in the center of an alder thicket. As their browsing circle had increased, the elk had trampled a small circle of cleared ground in the middle of the thicket. By spring, all the young alder shoots would be grazed flush and the elk'd have to move on.

They didn't have to worry much about predators. The wolves were down on the flats and bottoms, feeding on the frozen carcasses of the ranchers' cows. The coyotes, too. Only the mountain lion stayed up here all winter long, and it'd take a very brave or very hungry cat to jump into a little clearing where 20 full-grown elk waited to kick it to death.

Two does acted as sentries. They browsed on the outskirts of the herd, sniffing the air for any danger.

The wind was coming into Slocum's face—from the elk to him—and if the two hunters were slick enough, maybe they could get in closer.

The Indian signed that Slocum should lead the way, saying, in effect, "I've taken you this far. Now it's up to you."

Sure thing.

They were 100 feet above the thicket and perhaps 200 feet west of it. At that range, Slocum could have taken a couple of elk with the Colt, but he had other plans. He removed his snowshoes, eased down on his belly and slipped-slid down the slope, careful not to dislodge any snowballs. He moved like he had all the time in the world. Wordlessly, the Indian bellied down and followed.

They burrowed their way downslope to the edge of the thicket, moving so slow the elk didn't catch any sudden blur of movement.

Once they reached the alders, the elk were invisible, though Slocum could hear their stamping and munching and farting. Still on his belly, he slipped along through the thicket, hauling himself along by the alder clumps. The thick brush slid back easily over his coat. No whoosh, no scratching noises.

The Indian followed behind him, dead silent, like he was a ghost drifting over Slocum's trail. Slocum'd been followed by Indians a few times and never liked it. He didn't like it now.

The alders rose ten feet above them. From time to time a top would release a load of snow onto Slocum's head and neck. His gun hand was chilled clear through.

When he spotted the elk—dim shadows through the alders—he stopped and slipped his right hand into his groin. He was going to need that hand in the next few seconds and he'd have no need for his cock. Sweet Jesus, it was cold!

The nearest elk was 20 feet away, looking south, where the flight of a couple of ravens had attracted its attention. Slocum flagged the Indian back and eased forward through the snow.

The elk were busy about their business. Good-looking bunch, too: fat, sleek; the winter hadn't taken much out of them.

Just ahead, the snow dropped down onto the trampled, hardpacked surface of the elk yard. The nearest elk sentry was facing away from him now, watching the black ravens making lazy circles above the pines, crying out their caw, caw, caw. Very slowly, Slocum stood and walked forward into the middle of the elk herd. His rifle was held loosely in his right hand.

The Indian, behind him, didn't really believe what he was seeing. It had been a great bit of hunting to get so close to an elk yard without alerting the animals. And now this crazy white man was standing like a fool in the center of the herd with his rifle dangling from his hand. A great bit of hunting, but in a second the elk would scent him and the elk yard would explode.

Slocum was standing no more than five feet from the nearest feeding elk. The Indian watched with something like awe.

A young doe raised its head and looked Slocum right in the eye. For a moment it was real undecided: The sudden appearance of a human in the yard wasn't an everyday occurrence. Then it bleated, and every elk eye was on Slocum.

Slocum stood dead still.

The elk exploded, each of them making great leaps for the edge of the yard, scattering in every direction.

Baaraap! That's what Slocum's Colt sounded like to the Indian—like one shot—but it was five shots.

Slocum's first bullet took a lame, fat doe as it made its first (and last) jump. Took it high in the neck and broke it. Before the doe'd ended its leap in a broken heap, he'd picked his second shot—a young spike he meant for MacPherson—and the elk's spine was gone before it began its leap, while it was still hunkering.

Slocum took a brain shot at the sentry doe. There weren't any young ones hanging onto it. That was the longest shot, nearly 60 feet. The doe got two bounds before the back of its head flew away and it rolled against a great Douglas fir, legs thrashing.

Slocum hadn't liked the looks of one fawn: something spindly about its legs, and its rib cage was too prominent. It wouldn't make it through the winter. Slocum had to wait a split second while the two elk screening it got clear, and even then he couldn't see the whole fawn, so he broke its rear leg with one shot, and when it tumbled in the snow and came up again, he put his last shot through the heart.

Four elk were dead. The rest of them were crashing through the thicket. In a few seconds everything was quiet except for the ravens' cawing in the blue sky overhead.

Slocum had met a few people who just plain couldn't eat wild meat. Too bad. They'd eaten elk once or twice and, finding it too gamy, swore off. Slocum was a meat hunter and he knew the worst meat in the world was that of a trophy bull. "Hell," he'd said, "it's no better'n killin' a ten-year-old range bull and tryin' to eat that."

So he'd killed the young animals and let the big bucks go. He favored spikes (yearling bucks) because the herd didn't need but one to keep it in business. He'd kill a doe only if it wasn't going to breed right, or a fawn if it was too weak to make it.

After the kill, you had to care for the meat. You had to get the heat out of the carcass, and Slocum and the Indian proceeded to do just that. Somebody in Blue Rock had stolen Slocum's bowie knife from his gear, so all he had was a flat skinning knife, but it was razor-sharp. While he was slitting the bellies of the big doe and the fawn, the Indian was doing the same with the other two.

Slocum cut some travois poles and lashed them together with rawhide strips. They dragged the head-less, empty carcasses to the travois and tied them on.

The Indian was curious about the entrails. Slocum told him to take the small fawn and the lame doe. The Indian signed his thanks but picked through the guts for kidneys, livers and hearts. He took a bite of a heart and proffered it to Slocum. Slocum, ever polite, ripped off a chunk. He didn't much care for heart except in stews, but the hot flesh sent a shock through his body that he needed.

It was heavy work dragging the game out to Slocum's horse: The Indian couldn't pull his share, and they couldn't always choose the smoothest path, because of the awkward travois, and often they found themselves floundering hip deep in snow.

The winter light was fading when they reached the sled. The Indian signed his good-by. He'd hang most of his meat near here and carry one quarter home to his family.

"Your business," Slocum said. He handed the Indian a couple of extra lashings, fastened two elk to the sled and pulled out. He didn't want to be wandering around the mountains in the dark.

The light was almost gone by the time he hit the Blue Rock Trail, but the moon was bright enough to keep him out of trouble. He saw Walker's lights at the outskirts of town and headed for the saloon like a horse hurries home to the stable.

He tied his packhorse up and in a minute had a good offer for the doe: $20. He said they'd have to give a front quarter to the liveryman. Nobody objected.

Inside, he stamped the snow off his boots and nodded to Walker and the others. Walker was real interested in buying the spike buck, but Slocum said it was already taken.

"Well," Walker said, "let me buy you a drink anyway. The boys want to thank you for your round this morning."

Slocum didn't say anything. He drank his drink in peace.

It was cold outside. He'd done his work and now he was warm. Nothing else mattered.

5

Slocum was bone weary as he led his packhorse up the road to the mine manager's house. It had caught up with him. Around back, he found a small tool shed with the sort of overhanging roof he was looking for.

Lucia came out on the back porch and watched as he unlashed the spike, punched holes through its front tendons and lashed it to the roof peak, where the varmints wouldn't get it while it cooled.

87

Lucia's aristocratic face showed a little disdain at the dead animal hanging there, like it was somehow vulgar.

"Don't have to eat it if you don't want to," Slocum remarked. "You ain't on no hunger strike now."

She put her nose in the air and left Slocum to his work.

He peeled the skin away from the shanks until he had the front legs free. He was careful here: He didn't want to get elk hair on the meat, because that spoiled it sooner than anything. He made a pocket behind the animal's shoulders and shoved his hand in, making a fist, shoving, separating the skin from muscle as he went. Where the bones were close to the meat, he sliced the connecting membrane. In ten minutes or so the dead animal was . . . meat.

Slocum heard the thump of Pharoah MacPherson's wooden leg and nodded his hello. MacPherson was still in coveralls—dusty from the Britannia stamp mill—and he didn't want to touch the carcass, but he circled it approvingly.

"Damn fine-looking animal. Looks like I made a right decision turning you loose on our grocery problem."

"He'll be good meat," Slocum allowed.

"And as soon as I get cleaned up, I'll start cooking it."

Slocum thought the meat should hang overnight until it cooled and was easier to butcher, but he was pretty hungry and didn't object when the manager suggested they remove one ham for steaks. Slocum cut down to the hipbone, wrenched it back to break the cartilage and, with 50 pounds of meat slung over his shoulder, followed MacPherson into the kitchen.

After both men had washed up, the manager pulled chairs up to the fire and poured Slocum a snifter of brandy. "Cheers. And congratulations."

It was fine brandy. Better than he'd had last night.

"We never talked about your salary," the manager began.

"Salary" wasn't Slocum's favorite word. Hell, he wasn't going to get rich in Blue Rock anyway, so it didn't make much difference what the manager paid. "Board and room," Slocum said, "and I'll give you half price on the game I bring in. What you don't use, your miners will want."

Big smile from MacPherson. "Done!" he exclaimed, and clinked glasses to settle the bargain.

MacPherson as cook was as good as his word, and Slocum watched him cut thick steaks off the elk ham, pound them with the handle of a cleaver and dust them liberally with salt and pepper. Slocum liked watching a man do what he was good at, and the manager's enthusiasm was infectious.

"You know why America doesn't have a fine cuisine of its own?" MacPherson asked.

Slocum hadn't ever given it much thought one way or the other.

MacPherson grunted each time he whacked the elk steaks. "The ingredients are too good here," he said. "European cooks had to make do with inferior foods. They had to disguise them, don't you see. That's the secret to all those marvelous French stews: inferior meat, low-grade produce simmered and disguised and blended for hours. Now, there's not much a cook can do with elk meat. A little salt, a little pepper, sear it to retain the juices and serve it up. Spices? Who needs them."

"Uh-huh." Slocum had to smile at this strange one-legged man so particular about his stomach.

The steaks were juicy and delicious. They had bread smeared with lard, and canned tomatoes (the cowboy's friend). Slocum ate like he hadn't eaten in a long time, and nobody spoke much while they put themselves outside of a hearty meal.

Afterward, as Lucia leaned over to remove Slocum's plate, her breast brushed his arm in a way that wasn't

89

entirely accidental. "Opal won't dine with us tonight, Mr. Slocum. Her clothes are down at the livery stable and some family keepsakes, too. Trinkets, really, but she sets such a store on them."

"Uh-huh." Slocum didn't care too much where Opal was, but he'd take up Lucia's challenge later, not in front of her uncle.

"Elk ranches," the manager exclaimed. "That's what you Yanks need out here."

"It'd have to be a hell of a fence," Slocum observed laconically.

The manager waved away the difficulties with all the assurance of a man with a full gut, a glass of brandy and a fine Havana. "The Longhorn is doomed," he said. "They can survive on poor forage and defend themselves against predators, but their meat tastes like shoe leather and they don't gain rapidly. Hell, the meat's no good at all until the animal's four years old, and that's four winters to feed them."

Slocum knew that some cattlemen were importing native English beef—Herefords and Anguses—into the West. He talked about them with a cattleman's knowledge. He'd once rustled 300 of those very same imports, but he didn't feel obliged to mention that.

When Lucia rejoined them, she had a sparkle in her complexion that wasn't natural, and Slocum was flattered that she was showing off her beauty to him. She was a long-limbed thing: long-armed, long-legged. *Hell,* Slocum thought, *that girl'd wrap a man up tighter than a spider.* He got a hard-on thinking about it. And maybe she saw what was on his mind, for she blushed and hid her confusion in her glass.

She wore a gray gown—formal, severe even—that set off her angular figure. And the stays she wore under her bodice did nothing to hide the agitation of her heavy breasts.

What did she see when she looked at Slocum? A predator? A harsh man in a harsh land? A man tough as whang leather but able to observe all the small social graces with only a hint of the mockery he must have felt? Did she see a man who needed taming in the only way a man like him could be tamed—by a woman?

Perhaps he frightened her a little, because Lucia, who wasn't often rude, found herself asking, "How many men have you killed, Mr. Slocum?"

Slocum's grin was surprisingly boyish, still with that same overtone of mockery. "Only the ones that asked for it, ma'am," he drawled.

MacPherson was shocked at his niece's breach of courtesy and admonished her to remember her duty to their guest.

Maybe she would have obeyed, but Slocum was leaning back in his chair and grinning at her in the most infuriating manner. "Only those who asked for it, Mr. Slocum? And who decided that, pray?"

"Me."

"Who gave you the right to be judge, jury and executioner? Do you receive instructions directly from God, or do they arrive from a more, uh, temporal realm?"

Slocum was tired of it. "How many men has Queen Victoria had killed? How about General Grant, or any other general you might name? Well, we ain't got no kings or queens or generals out here to tell us who to kill, so most of us have to do the decidin' ourselves."

Pharoah MacPherson guffawed and refilled Slocum's glass. "I believe he's got you there, my dear. Yes, I believe Mr. Slocum's had the best of it."

"Nonsense!" she snapped. Her hands clinked the bottle against the lip of her glass. She was a little red in the face. "Tell me, Mr. Slocum," she asked sweetly, "what do you think about women?"

"Never knew what to think."

"What do you think about women's rights? The vote?"

Slocum reached into the mahogany humidor, selected a long Havana, bit the end, spat and handed her the cigar. "Don't waste it," he said. "It's good tobacco."

91

She stared at the cigar in her hand like it was some sort of snake.

Slocum was running an experiment. Out here some of the saloon girls smoked cigars. Calamity Jane and Doc Holiday's whore, "Big-Nose" Kate, smoked cigars. Ladies did not smoke and referred to smoking as "that filthy habit." Slocum wondered what the London ladies did.

"Match," Lucia said.

A surprised MacPherson handed her a sulphur match.

In a mock-mannish way, she dragged the match over the sole of her shoe, balancing like a one-legged heron. She created a dense cloud of blue smoke.

MacPherson's mouth was agape.

Lucia said, "Equal rights for women, Mr. Slocum, are determined by more important considerations than any woman's ability to smoke cigars." She coughed very slightly. She coughed like she wanted to cough more but was choking it back, and Slocum grinned because he knew she was just trying to make a point and wasn't going to get to make it, because her skin was going from pink to green.

"Women's rights," she stated. She became alarmed, stopped her statement and glared.

"You were saying?"

Slocum was grinning this most infuriating grin; he would not be tamed. Her stomach was trying to send her a message, though her pride was urging her to ignore it. "Excuse me," she said. She left the room, puffing determinedly on the cigar, trailing smoke behind her like a steamship in still air.

The two men heard the back door slam behind her and the sound of retching.

"Waste of a fine meal," MacPherson sighed. "Slocum, are you always this antagonistic? My niece is a fine woman."

"I'm only antagonistic to fine women," Slocum said. "Only kind that's worth it."

And they sipped on their brandy and were content to sit in comfortable silence.

Lucia went around the long way to get upstairs. Embarrassment, Slocum guessed. Too bad. He was having a pretty good time, and she was a startlingly good-looking woman.

Slocum and MacPherson talked, as old warriors will after a good meal and a couple of glasses of brandy. They talked about friends who had fallen. They talked about the "Wild Geese," those Irish soldiers of fortune who officered most of the frontier regiments.

Slocum spoke about Captain Miles Keogh, the last and bravest of the men killed at the Little Big Horn.

MacPherson reminisced about the Crimea: that deadly, comic-opera war. He talked knowledgeably on that war's great killers: cholera, infections and diphtheria. Puffing his cigar, he eyed Slocum curiously. "I notice you don't wear a sidearm," he said.

Slocum liked and trusted MacPherson (as much as he trusted anyone). He wondered what the old warrior would say if he admitted that he was a pacifist—for the next eight months anyway. But Slocum knew if word got out that he couldn't use a six-gun, his life wouldn't be worth a nickel. Every two-bit tinhorn and would-be gunsel in the territory would think him fair game. There were more than a few fools who'd like to be "the man who shot John Slocum." So he kept his secret. He said, "No, I haven't been wearing a short gun recently." He laughed. "Too many fast kids around."

MacPherson thought he wouldn't want to be one of those fast kids.

The smoke curled up lazily from their cigars to gather under the high white plaster ceiling and mingle with the aroma of the brandy. It was getting on to nine o'clock.

MacPherson snapped his gold hunter closed and announced that he had a busy day planned tomorrow. They'd found a rich dike of ore and he had to be on the spot constantly, because his miners weren't above a little high-grading. "Hell"—he laughed—"some of my Cornishmen would make more out of a rich find than the owners would unless I watch them like a hawk."

"Opal's late," Slocum observed.

MacPherson looked sad. "Perhaps she had second thoughts about Sheriff Hammer. Perhaps she prefers living with him to being Lucia's housemaid."

Slocum grunted. Her business.

But later, as he laid the blankets on the couch in the large quiet room, he thought about Opal and was a little worried. The girl was playing in a rough game. She didn't really know how rough.

Slocum was wrong: Opal had a very good idea how rough the game was and how terrifying. At this moment, she would have given ten years of her life to be in Slocum's arms. Instead, she was crouched, scared witless, between two barrels of scrap outside the blacksmith shop, and the silent killers were searching for her.

She didn't dare scream. They'd never been far enough away for her to scream. If they found her, they'd kill her in an instant.

It started simply enough. George Ives had tossed her meager belongings into the mud in front of Walker's, announcing to the guffawing miners, "She ain't gonna let me have her ass; I ain't gonna cover it with pretties. Let Slocum dress the goods he's got the usin' of."

Funny joke. After the miners went back inside, the black liveryman gathered her pitiful belongings in a gunny sack. He'd been poor himself often enough and had a good idea how much the scruffy pile of clothes and trinkets meant to the girl. He sent a terse note to MacPherson's house. In his heavy block handwriting, he told her where she could reclaim her belongings.

Opal wanted her mother's silver brooch and the family testament that had been in the Hevener family as long as anyone could remember, so she went out of the

94

MacPherson house as soon as the liveryman's note was delivered. She stopped at the general store and bought some soap, a pack of pins (she intended doing a little repair work on a few salvageable dresses) and some black and white thread. She also bought herself three cents' worth of horehound drops because she had an incurable sweet tooth.

It was dusk. She'd have to be getting home soon. Already the miners were inside Walker's or eating dinner at the rooming house; the smells of cooking drifted across the town.

Opal intended a quick stop, a thank you to the liveryman and home to a quiet evening (and maybe a night with Slocum). She was thinking about Slocum as she entered the livery. Opal Hevener was wondering if just maybe she was falling in love.

Pure foolishness, she thought. *That man isn't gonna hold still or wait for no woman, much as she'd want him to. And he's probably had a sight of them ask.*

The stable was quiet. A few horses chewing and belching. No sign of the liveryman. Opal called out, "Hey, you in there?" and a horse looked up from its stall for a moment before it resumed eating.

"Liveryman," Opal called out. She heard nothing but the quiet living sounds of the horses. She walked back into the stable. She knew the liveryman slept back here somewhere, but she didn't quite know where. Some of the townspeople claimed he slept in a stall with the horses.

The horses' body heat warmed the stable some, and Opal couldn't see her breath anymore as she slipped quietly past the stalls.

He was in the very last stall. Opal thought for a moment he might be sleeping, but as soon as she saw all of him, sprawled out the way he was, she knew. She didn't really need to bend over and examine him, but she bent anyway. He'd been her friend, and she didn't have too many friends in Blue Rock.

The black man's throat was cut—cut so savagely

that his head was lying floppy on his neck and the white bone of the vertebrae showed above the pool of rich purple blood staining the hay. His teeth were showing in a mockery of a grin, and his hair was loose and wild where the murderer had grabbed it, the better to butcher him by.

Opal had seen death before. But the brutality of the liveryman's murder sickened her and scared her, too. She raised her eyes wildly and saw them coming for her between the stalls.

"No!" she said.

Maybe her voice was too choked to be heard, or maybe they just didn't care, because they kept on coming. One of them grinned, and his grin was the same grin the stableman had, and on a living face it looked twice as awful.

She ran. The stable had no back door, she knew—the back of the livery faced Blue Rock Creek, and as the liveryman used to say, "No sense puttin' a door back there for the fishes"—so she ran right at them, not as a frightened girl runs but full tilt, a terrified wild animal, and though they were very confident, though they reached out to grasp her, at the last possible moment she dove right at their legs. The impact knocked the wind out of her, but she was up again quick, somehow avoiding their clutching hands.

Behind her, they were cursing as they thrashed around in the dimness, and she ran even faster, not minding the smears on her gingham dress, just running, running for her life.

She slammed the door behind her and looked for something—a rock, a log—to roll against it, but they'd recovered from their surprise and were coming after her, so she whimpered "Oh, my God" and bolted around the corner of the livery, hoping they'd think she was crossing the main street and lose precious seconds scanning the muddy thoroughfare for her slight fleeing form.

Opal Hevener was a civilized woman, more educated than an Apache squaw, with better manners than the African natives she used to support when the mission contributions were taken at the Piney Hill Baptist Church back home. But the glaze of civilization, as any soldier knows, is a superficial one, and Opal was moving now like a woman who'd never learned the difference between "ain't" and "am not" or how to write (in clumsy block printing) her own name.

And, she was young. She was as agile as a tomboy, and the rigors of her life had made her soft woman's muscles a little harder than those of her eastern cousins. Like an animal she moved: quick around the corner of the livery; quick along the beaten path between the livery and the forge next door.

The light was almost gone. Everyone in Blue Rock was inside, snug against the bitter cold. The bright yellow squares of their windows—behind which they talked or ate their supper—looked terribly appealing to her.

She couldn't outrun her pursuers on the straightaway, and if she got too far ahead, she supposed they'd shoot her. Somehow she had to keep their hopes up while contriving to return to MacPherson's home—the only protection this town offered her, now or ever.

When she guessed her pursuers were out of the stable, she flung herself between two barrels of clinkers from the forge and huddled into a small ball. The smith had been shoeing today and the warmth of the fire was still in some of the clinkers and the smell of the charcoal, too. Opal didn't notice the smell, but the slight warmth slipped right through her lightweight dress and she was grateful for it.

She heard the crunch of footsteps in the alleyway. *Let them go away, Lord,* she prayed. *Let them think I went the other direction. Let me live, Lord, and I'll never do anything bad in my life again and I'll even write my Aunt Dorrie.*

But, apparently, Providence was indifferent to the

state of Aunt Dorrie's correspondence, because the footsteps kept advancing: slow, deliberate, cautious.

Opal was thinking, and that was her mistake. When she had reacted on the animal level, all her moves had worked. Now, in her fear, with the fear sweat drying in the cold, she was thinking, and her mind wasn't half so good as her body's reflexes. *One more step closer,* she thought; *when I hear the next step, I'll run.*

They weren't talking. The slow crunch, crunch, crunch of their footsteps unnerved her more than any threats or curses would have done. She bolted.

They had been ready to quit, convinced that she must be around the other side of the building or that she'd found shelter and right now was pouring her story (and their future) into some amazed miner's ears, and they almost didn't see her. In the dim light, it looked like a quick, furry animal had darted from between the barrels and rushed around the corner.

She'd lost her main chance—her last chance. Though she ran and hid, ducked and darted, one of them was always right behind her and the other somewhere about, blocking her escape. They chivied her through the snow like cowboys herding a jumpy mustang. Their hearts weren't beating like they wanted to explode. Their feet weren't great awkward weights on the end of their legs. Now they moved with confidence, ready to finesse her into a corner from which there was no retreat. She'd been heading uphill, toward the Britannia. One of them held a gun and let her see it. The slight gleam of the revolver barrel almost blinded her, it was so bright. She sobbed, "Please."

But her little girl's voice and her little girl's plea didn't slow them. They came on, bracketing her between them, moving slowly, deliberate as death after a long sickness.

Though her heart was pounding and she couldn't see much through the blur of her tears, she ducked at the last minute and, her breath sobbing through her tortured lungs, ran for the Britannia mill.

Only a little farther, only a little farther, the words ran through her mind, and maybe they helped, because her feet were driving up the hill through the snow and the men hadn't caught her yet. She ran through the main door of the mill, dropped the crossbar in place and leaned against the door, sobbing and trying to catch her breath.

The mill was empty, and the huge machines—the stamp, the settling tanks, the concentrator and the long ore tables—looked like relics to her, artifacts from a civilization of trolls and giants. The peaked roof was 100 feet above her, crisscrossed with beams and rafters. The floor beneath her feet was packed earth.

It wouldn't be long before they broke in. One wall of the mill was all glass, and there were other doors.

She found refuge in MacPherson's office. She jammed herself behind a wooden case of maps and files. The case was oak, about eight feet tall, with a two-foot gap between it and the wall. She squeezed herself in there and listened.

She couldn't run anymore. Her legs were gone, her wind was gone, she was driven to ground.

She heard their steps. Her heart plummeted and she sent off another prayer—no words this time, no appeal, just naked need and fear and helplessness.

But Providence didn't hear her this time, either.

The footsteps faded. For a long, long time she didn't hear anything but the tortured rasp of her own breathing. Then, a scuffling sound. *Maybe it's just a rat,* she thought. *Just a rat.*

She wanted to cough, and pressed her finger against her throat to suppress the cough. It worked. She wondered if she could stay here until morning, motionless, silent as a mouse. The mill wasn't heated: She might freeze. *Better to freeze to death than be caught,* she thought.

It'd been half an hour since she heard the scuffling sound, and once more hope was beginning to dawn in

99

her, when a hand reached around the side of the cabinet and grabbed her hair.

She would have screamed then, but they covered her mouth. One held a 14-inch bowie, still red from the liveryman's throat; the other held a Colt. There was nothing she could do; no way she could run or hide.

Opal was strangely docile now, all the fight gone out of her. She'd given it her best.

She didn't struggle when they hauled her out of the office. They dragged her beside the stamp, its 20-ton piston lost high above them in the shadows under the ceiling. She didn't fight when they ripped off her gingham dress, though it was the only really good dress she owned and she'd hoped to impress Lucia Mac-Pherson with it, because she wanted to be friends. She didn't fight when he pushed her to her knees and opened his pants.

He used her. He used her like she'd never been used. He hurt her.

It was only when they shoved her bleeding, naked body onto the stamp bed and pressed her face into the grit of the pulverized rock that she screamed.

6

Slocum sat bolt upright, Opal's scream still ringing in his ears. It was a scream of mortal terror and cut through the cold air like a blade.

Whump! The tremendous crash of the 20-ton stamp as it hit the steel platform cut off the scream, though somehow it continued to echo in his ears.

Softly he padded to the window and looked out at the smooth, silent snow and the bulk of the stamp mill, only 100 yards away. The sweat was running down his face, but he didn't pay it any mind. He pulled on his pants and boots and was out the door, running toward the mill through the snow. He slipped and went to his knees twice but didn't notice; if you'd asked him after-

ward, he wouldn't have remembered. He wore no
jacket against the weather. The main door was locked,
so he went around the side of the mill where the tall,
strange windows overlooked the town like the cold
eyes of some watchful king.

Slocum made a fist and punched the glass, and
though he cut his knuckles some, it wasn't too bad and
he plucked the shards out of the window frame before
pulling his hand back past their jagged menace. He
slipped through the small, nasty hole and landed on the
mill floor. Except for the single crash of the breaking
window, he hadn't made a sound. Silently he padded
through the mill. The only light was moonlight reflected
off the snow. It poured through the windows and cast
the machines into incredible, bizarre shapes. Though
he couldn't hear a damn thing, his nose picked up the
unmistakable odors of sex and blood. *Like an orgy in
a slaughterhouse,* he thought as he padded from shadow
to shadow.

He found Opal. He found part of Opal, anyway. Her
body dangled like a ruptured sausage out of the stamp
mill. The steel stamp had flattened the upper half of
her. He didn't recognize the body though he'd known
it and held it. He recognized the torn gingham dress
lying beside the stamp. He melted into the shadows
again, waiting for the murderers to make their next
move.

They were gone. In a moment of listening, he knew
it. He saw lights outside the mill. Opal's rescuers were
a little late.

The procession of lanterns reminded Slocum of the
Penitentes in New Mexico. Not many white men had
ever seen the long line of Flagellants as they made their
agonizing way deep into the Sierra Madre Mountains
and lived to tell about it. Slocum wondered if he'd
outlive this particular procession.

They shouted to one another. They didn't know what
was waiting for them in the tall, cold mill and they'd
come into pistol range. Slocum watched them dashing

101

from snowbank to snowbank, seeking cover. One good Colt and he could have killed five of them fast as he could roll the hammer.

When he stepped back from the windows, the bright moonlight sent his shadow darting against the huge mining machines like a demented moth.

Slocum was looking for evidence. He figured George for the killer, but he wanted more than his own say-so. The miners knew George. Some liked him. They wouldn't take Slocum's word without proof.

All the mining machines were big and simple. With the exception of the steam engine that lifted the giant stamp, most of them had been assembled on the premises. Slocum checked under each of the ore tables. He peered into the concentrator tub. He found a couple of mashed cigarette butts near Opal's dress, but they didn't prove much. Slocum's long legs moved him through the shadowy mill like he was gliding on ball bearings.

A voice outside: "Josey, you take the back."

And someone, Josey presumably, called back, "I ain't goin' up there alone. I heard that scream. Somethin' awful's happened in there and I don't want it happenin' to me."

That's right, Josey, Slocum thought. *You be cautious: You'll live longer that way.*

Slocum was running out of time. He had only a few more seconds before some miner, bolder than the rest, decided to break into the mill. Slocum knew what they'd think if they caught him in here with Opal's body. Dead to rights, that's what they'd think.

He slipped into MacPherson's office like a gray, silent wraith. The manager's desk had been pushed aside; some reports and journals were strewn on the floor, and *The Compendium of Metals* had been hurled halfway across the room. Slocum sniffed and he didn't have to look any further. Opal's scent, and the scent of her fear. Maybe something else, too: tears?

How terrified she must have been, Slocum thought.

He could smell male sweat, too. The room stank of it, like a stallion stinks of lust and nervous energy. The smell was so rich and so strong, he couldn't make out whether there'd been one man or two.

Well, he'd cut it fine enough. A moment ago he'd heard the rattle of the front-door latch, and Josey'd be around back if he'd managed to get a few brave souls to accompany him.

Lanterns shone in the front windows of the mill and a few white faces were pressed against the glass, their eyes shaded against their own lanterns' glare. Slocum didn't spare them a thought. The reflection off the glass would blind an Indian. He made a beeline for a small door at the rear of the building that looked little used. As he lifted the crossbar on the door, somebody broke out a pane of glass behind him. There was no reason he didn't sense the men waiting outside that door. No reason at all.

Slocum got over his surprise before the miner did. The miner opened his mouth to yelp. Slocum closed it for him with the crossbar and swung the door shut again. The miner's partner was yelling, "Hey, he's here! We found him! He's killed Josey!"

Slocum hadn't, but Josey would need to see a dentist before he could chew dried beef again.

Slocum ran across the floor top speed, hoping to find another bolt hole. If the miners caught him here, there weren't any explanations he could make. He passed one door, already shuddering as the miners threw themselves against it. He saw the gleam of a lantern, heard the excited babble of voices and the snick, snick, snick as the miners checked their guns.

Damn! Once they found Opal's body, they'd shoot on sight. Slocum peered up at the rafters and stringers far overhead. He sprang to the lip of the concentrator tub and, hand over hand, shinnied himself up. In half a second he was crouched on a 6′ x 6′ timber as the lanterns streamed by beneath. Once they passed, he'd just drop down behind them and out the door and gone.

103

X. Beidler's voice: "I want two men posted by each door. If anyone tries to leave, don't ask questions. Shoot."

Slocum padded along the stringers, restless, prowling, looking for a way out.

Somebody cried, "Over here! Jesus Christ, somebody get over here!" The voice became a screech: "Mr. B-B-Beidler!"

So: They'd found Opal.

Slocum was watching the doors, but the guards Beidler had posted on the doors weren't going to budge.

Someone was yelling, "Who in the hell could have done a thing like this?"

And somebody else was vomiting.

Beidler shouted for the men at the doors to stay at their posts or, by God, he'd have their hides. Slocum watched the guards' lanterns draw closer together.

The 6' x 6' stringers were held together by wooden headers, so the entire loft of the mill was connected in a grid. Slocum slipped along easily toward the tall cylinder of the steam boiler and the massive stamp mill. He walked upright and silent, his feet sure on the narrow beam.

Below, the miners had formed a semicircle around the girl's body and several of them had removed their stiff felt hats. One or two crossed themselves, but they didn't make much of it, because they were Irish Catholics trying to pass as Cornishmen. They were very quiet. Awed, almost.

One young miner whispered, "Women are scarce as hen's teeth out here. Why'd somebody want to go and mash such a pretty one?" Maybe he spoke for them all.

Slocum hunkered down on his heels and made a point of not staring at any one man. He didn't want to alert the animal sense we all have when somebody is eyeing us out of the darkness.

The miners were scared: Maybe the killer was still in the building. Nervously, the miners on the edge of

104

the circle kept trying to push to the inside, and the men on the inside kept elbowing them back.

"God damn it," Beidler roared, "stop jostling each other! You got guns, don't you? You know how to use them? Everybody fan out through the building and we'll catch the son of a bitch who did this and make him pay for it."

Slocum wasn't the son of a bitch Beidler was talking about, but he'd do in a pinch.

"Now, damn it," Beidler went on, "don't go shootin' holes in each other. You make sure you know who you got in your sights before you crank one off. Any man who shoots without good cause will answer to me."

Some of the men scuffed their feet and some nodded and some started moving through the darkened mill. From above, Slocum watched their progress.

They searched where he'd searched. Different groups went over the same ground time and again. Beidler was in MacPherson's office. Like Slocum, he'd smelled something wrong among the tattered mining periodicals and the shabby furniture. Slocum hoped he'd find something concrete: something that didn't point to John Slocum.

Two burly miners had abandoned the search to gawk at the girl's corpse. One of them fired up a cheroot and flipped his match at Opal's foot.

"Don't do that."

"Why not? She can't feel it. Maybe you just don't want the goods more damaged than they already are. Don't worry. All the essential parts are still there."

One man knelt to peer at her. "Damn, she was pretty, wasn't she? If I wasn't a picky sort of man, I swear I'd give her a try right now."

The other man sneered. "Better'n the Chinaman, eh, boy?"

"What Chinaman?"

"Ain't you heard? The Chinaman who's got the claim below Jackson's. Six bucks."

"That's a lot of money for a Chinaman."

"Oh, he don't get but a dollar of it. The five's for the two men who hold him. He don't like it."

When Jim Thiel joined the two men, they stopped their joking. Thiel was sober-faced as he looked at the girl, shook his head and said, "This is a hell of a thing. Just a hell of a thing. I been thinkin' about leavin' this town and I'm decided now." He made a gesture of disgust. "This! I got a decent grubstake put together and I'm goin' back to Pennsylvania. Coal mines. There's nothin' like this back there. They're *civilized* men."

One of the other men grunted, "Yeah, sure."

Thiel bent over and inspected the stamp. The stamp wasn't quite flat on the table. Heavy as it was, the ore stamp should have liquified anything as soft as human bone and settled flat against its striking surface. "Boys," Thiel said, "I think there's somethin' in here."

"Course there is. And I sure as hell don't want to look close at it. I got a delicate stomach."

"No. Not her. Somethin' steel. Peer in there, why don't you. It's lyin' in there about three feet. The stamp's restin' on it."

One of them shouted for Beidler, and the dusty vigilante came over at a trot.

The easy way to retrieve the object—and what remained of Opal Hevener's torso and head—was to raise the stamp with steam, but the steam engine was dead cold. Somebody went off to fetch Pharoah Mac-Pherson. The others debated the merits of unbolting the stamp. Some wanted to pry it up with bars. Beidler was shaking his head no. "The bars will bend," he said. "We have no bars strong enough to lift twenty tons without bending."

Thiel settled the matter when he brought over four heavy steel chocks and a 30-pound sledge. The chocks were wedge-shaped and six inches wide at the big end. He placed them around the stamp, points in, spat on his hands and made his heavy hammer ring. He swung three times at each chock before he moved to the next one, and bit by bit the stamp lifted up.

An eager miner slid his hand under there.

"You stupid bastard," Thiel yelled, "use a bar! Sweep it out! You want to lose your arm?"

But the man already had what he wanted. His arm was wet with red blood and some white and gray matter it didn't pay to think about or identify. He peeled off his shirt, wiped his gory arm and tossed his shirt on the floor like he didn't need it anymore, though it was −10° and him in his union suit.

Released from the pinch of the stamp, Opal Hevener slid out of the machine that had killed her.

The men looked away. One vomited. Slocum closed his eyes until she'd plopped on the floor.

"What did you find, man?" Beidler snapped.

The miner held up a metal object about 14 inches long. It may have been shiny once. It wasn't now. It was a bowie knife. Though the haft had been flattened slightly, Slocum knew the lettering on the butt would still be legible. He would have bet $100 he knew what the lettering said: "J.S."

Too bad. It'd been a fine knife.

The man wiped the knife on Opal Hevener's best dress and hefted it for balance.

"Could be they cut her throat before they tripped the stamp," Thiel suggested.

"It's possible," Beidler said. He wasn't interested in the details of death, only in assigning the blame for it.

Thiel found the initials on the butt and read them aloud, and a low murmur went through the crowd as they figured out whose knife it was.

Slocum would have won his $100: The initials were "J.S.," all right. Slocum rose off his haunches and glided away from there. It was time for him to make himself scarce—unless he wanted to shake hands with the devil.

One of the guards on the front door was edging away from his post. He wanted to hear what was being said near the girl's body. His partner, a bony kid with a large Adam's apple, was whining at him, "Stick closer, Buck. Mr. Beidler'd have our hides if we was to let the killer get by us."

Slocum walked directly over their heads. He was figuring his chances. He thought he could flatten the kid and be out the door before Buck or any other reinforcements arrived. He sprang.

Wrong again.

One of his boot heels was a little loose and a little twisted; a tiny piece of leather caught the edge of the beam, and what was meant to be a smooth, even dive became an awkward, sprawling thing. Slocum meant to land on the kid like a panther, but he hit like a blanket falling off a wash line.

The kid's shoulder caught him just under the rib cage. Sure the kid went down, but Slocum went down, too, wheezing for breath.

When Slocum hit him, the kid let out a yelp, and Buck was back before Slocum could get up again. He was on his knees when Buck's rifle smacked him across the base of the spine and hurled him forward, away from the door, and good old Buck was squalling at the top of his lungs, "I got him! I got him here! For God's sake, get over here before he kills the two of us!" He swung his rifle like a bat at Slocum's midsection.

Half a dozen men came running toward him. The kid and Buck were between him and the door. And he was breathing like an asthmatic old woman. Slocum said, "Goddammit to hell," lunged for the top of a partition, balanced for a second, then sprang upward for the safety of the rafters.

He moved so fast that those who might have thought about shooting didn't think, and those who were ready to shoot never had a good target.

The rafters and headers hung suspended above the mill floor like a great wooden web. Twenty feet up in the darkness, Slocum was invisible. A few men fired anyway. The gunshots roared in the cavernous mill like thunderclaps, but the bullets came nowhere near him and went on to punch holes in the mill's tin roof.

"Goddammit!" Beidler yelled. "Hold your fire! You're shootin' at shadows. I want some men up there, right now!"

The miners were none too eager. And when Beidler announced that they should leave their six-guns below so they wouldn't shoot one another in the darkness, his corps of volunteers shrank even further.

Lots of muttering and a few angry boasts and, finally, a few miners started climbing the big machines. Slocum spotted them by the lanterns of their ever-helpful friends. He waited near the center of the web like an angry spider. He was nursing his sore body and cursing his damn bad luck.

The men fanned out through the rafters, calling encouragement to one another: "Watch over to your left, Bill. You don't want him comin' up on your blind side."

"Watch your own self, you damn fool."

Slocum never fought on a tightrope before. He set his back against a broad upright and waited.

The cry went up: "I see him—over there in the middle! He ain't got no gun. You all be careful."

They made a loose circle around their prey and started edging closer. One of the wiser heads was calling for a gun. "I can see him clear. I can blow him right off of there!" he shouted.

But Slocum was already in motion, running along the narrow beams straight at his tormentors. He wasn't about to let them get set.

When he saw Slocum coming, the nearest man jumped ship. He landed on a few of his friends. They cushioned his fall.

Slocum's punch sent the next man squalling. When two men came at him from front and back, he slipped one off his shoulders and kicked him before smashing the other right between the eyes. They wobbled off into space.

109

And then there were three: one riding his back, one flailing at his belly and the third punching past his partner whenever he saw an opening.

The man on Slocum's back was riding him like a horse and kicking the hell out of his legs. Slocum dropped to one knee to dislodge him, but he would not let go. Slocum swept one long arm in front of him and dumped an attacker off the beam. A wail. A thud. The next man kicked at him, and Slocum grabbed his heel and tossed him after his friend.

More men piled on, and though the narrow beam didn't let anybody get in a real good lick, they were doing their damnedest.

Somebody was hammering on Slocum's ear. The face swimming before him was red and sweaty, and Slocum punched it out of the way. He still had one man on his back, so Slocum ran him against an upright until the man turned loose and fell away.

Somebody got in a good shot at Slocum's ribs. Somebody was hitting him over the head. He grabbed hold of a fat miner's shirt and twisted. He wanted something soft to land on. The fat miner wasn't all that soft, and when Slocum hit the floor, he blacked out.

He dreamed. He dreamed about Little Round Top. The crazy colonel led the charge into his own bank. Slocum wanted to help but couldn't, because he had no gun. The colonel was grinning at him.

John Slocum opened his eyes.

"Welcome back to the land of the living," X. Beidler said calmly. "Why don't a couple of you boys take Mr. Slocum's arms."

A couple of big miners hoisted Slocum to his feet. They weren't too gentle. Slocum was weak. He waited for his vision to clear.

X. Beidler—pale, dusty, composed—was smoking the remnants of a once-proud cigar. He stared at Slocum like a cattle buyer at an auction. He rocked back on his heels. He rocked forward again. He was making Slocum dizzy.

"What's a nice boy like you doin' in a place like this?" Slocum rasped.

Beidler's eyebrows went up. "You make jokes? At a time like this?"

"Anyone can make jokes when they're happy."

Slocum caught a blur of movement behind him. Someone was going to club him into submission, but Beidler shook his head no.

"I heard you were a bad man," Beidler said. "I heard you were pretty handy with a Colt. I heard you weren't the best man to hire to guard a bank vault. But, hell"—he gestured toward Opal Hevener's mutilated body—"I never heard nothin' *real* bad about you."

"I never killed her," Slocum said. He thought he'd say the words even though they wouldn't do him much good. "I heard her scream and the noise of that damn stamp mill and came over here, same as you."

"Yes," Beidler said. He didn't mean yes.

Slocum's arms hurt. "Why don't you call off your apes?" he said. "I can stand by myself."

"I'm sure you can," Beidler said, "but you are a very dangerous man and I am inclined to be cautious. Set him back on that nail keg, boys. You don't have to hold him tight, but don't let go of him."

"You know who did this," Slocum said. "You know it was George Ives and Hammer killed this girl. She was movin' out and they couldn't stand it."

"Yes," Beidler said. He didn't mean yes this time, either.

Well, what the hell. If they were determined to hang him, there wasn't much Slocum could do about it. He'd never begged a man for his life, and now was a little late in the day to start.

"You're quite a lawman, Beidler," Slocum said. "I heard a few things about you, too. I heard you like to see people dancin' in the sky. I heard that old Shotgun Slade's in Chicago now. I heard he draws a real good crowd. You ever see him? Floatin' in that big green

111

bottle with his hair like seaweed. How many innocent men you strung up?"

There was the faintest touch of color in X. Beidler's face as he said, "I have no business with the innocent." Then he smiled and Slocum wished he hadn't because he'd seen a few skulls with the smile Beidler was wearing. Beidler stretched, shaking the stiffness out of his compact body. He reached inside his coat. He said, "Cigar?"

"Sure. Why not?"

But Beidler didn't bring out a Havana. His hand was holding Slocum's bowie, wrapped in a scrap of gingham cloth. He unwrapped the knife, held it to the light and inspected the initials. "I believe this is yours?"

"Yeah, it's mine. Someone stole it off my packhorse while I was in the hoosegow."

"Two murders, Slocum: the liveryman and the girl."

"You mentioned a cigar," Slocum said.

Beidler grabbed at his pocket and tossed Slocum a smoke.

Deliberately, sensuously, Slocum licked it and sniffed at it before he lit up. "Not bad," he said. He crossed his legs and lounged on the nail keg like he didn't have a care in the world. But John Slocum's eyes were constantly scanning the men around him, looking for the one chance that'd get him out of this fix.

Beidler smiled his skull smile. "Enjoy your cigar, Slocum," he said. "Please do enjoy your cigar."

Suddenly the cigar didn't taste very good. It tasted like the dirt from a freshly dug grave.

The miners were getting impatient. It was cold. It was late. It was going to be a rough day for the working man tomorrow after staying up half the night.

Someone said: "He killed her! Let's string him up and go home."

Another voice said: "He done it. Make him pay."

One man was coiling a rope. He had a vivid bruise on his face, so maybe his motive for wanting Slocum dead was somewhat personal. He was twisting the rope back and forth in his gnarled hands like he was wringing it dry. Slocum couldn't keep his eyes off it.

"Hell," Slocum said, "give Beidler a little time. It ain't every day a man's got to make up his mind to commit murder."

A few men growled at Slocum's remark. The cry went up again for a speedy resolution.

Beidler's sigh sounded like air rushing out of a child's balloon. He crushed out his cigar. When his eyes looked at Slocum, they were puzzled and sad. "I never would have figured it of you," he said. Then he barked an order. "Charlie! Loop the noose over those rafters. Make sure it's running free."

Slocum watched as Charlie tossed the noose a couple of times until he had it over the rafters. It hung like it was something dangerous—and of course it was.

"Very well," Beidler snapped. "You all know this man. You all knew the victims. You've all seen this knife—Slocum's knife. Slocum says he didn't kill either of the victims. What's your verdict: guilty or no?"

Most of the miners looked around to see what their neighbors were going to say, then uttered a ragged chorus of "Guilty."

"And those who say no?"

Thiel spoke his "No" loud and clear. Slocum thanked him with a glance. There was a silence, broken only by the scuffling of boots and the sniveling of a man who had a cold. "And I too say 'No,' " Beidler said.

A brief mutter from the miners.

"But I will abide by the will of the majority," Beidler continued. "John Slocum, you have been judged guilty of murder by a jury of your peers. You got anything to say before we string you up?"

"Sure: Fuck you."

Someone coughed. They were pushing Slocum toward the rope, and his eyes were still flickering around, looking for that one slim chance he needed. They pulled the heavy noose over his head and set the knot behind his neck so it'd break clean. A couple of men went into MacPherson's office to get a chair for Slocum to stand on. John Slocum wasn't thinking about anything. He was singing his death song.

"What the hell is going on?" Pharoah MacPherson was pushing through the crowd, his brows drawn tight and his pale-blue eyes flashing. "What the hell do you dumb muckers think you're doing?"

Lucia was right on his heels, her face white and set, her eyes on the rope around Slocum's neck. The miners parted before her. Some said "Ma'am"; some removed their hats.

"Take that rope off him," MacPherson ordered. Magically, an aisle formed in the crowd between the angry manager and the dusty little German. "You!" MacPherson snapped. "What are you doing in my mill?"

Beidler shrugged. He pointed at the stamp mill. MacPherson looked puzzled until he saw Opal Hevener's body. He opened his mouth and closed it again. His face was linen white.

Lucia stood up on tiptoes to see. She said, *"Oh";* then, in a small, thin voice, she said "Excuse me" and knelt by the remains of her friend. When she lifted her head, her eyes were vacant and wandering. "Why?" she said.

Somebody coughed.

MacPherson snapped, "Get that rope off him! I won't have it. You men are trespassing. This is my mill. If you don't clear out of here in five minutes, don't bother to show up for work tomorrow."

The miners nearest MacPherson tried to melt into the crowd. The men behind them pushed them back into the limelight.

Beidler explained about the knife. Calmly he pointed to the fatal initials. Very slowly he drew his belly gun. He wasn't exactly pointing it at MacPherson, but he wasn't pointing it away, either. "I'd hate to be the man to stand between me and my duty," he said. His voice was $-20°$.

Lucia got to her feet. She was a little weak in the knees, but her voice was steady enough. "But you can't hang him. He's an innocent man."

A few men looked away. A few others found it was a good time to cough or spit.

"Please," she begged. "He's innocent. You don't want to have his murder on your consciences."

"Lucia!" Slocum snapped. "Get off your damn knees! If they're gonna hang me, they're gonna."

"Ma'am," Beidler said gently, "you go on home now. There's no reason for you to watch this."

"But he's an innocent man. He didn't kill her."

Beidler was a little aggravated. "Sure. Now, why do you say that?"

Lucia swallowed hard. She searched Slocum's impassive face. "Because," she said, "because when that stamp fell, just after that horrible scream, he . . . he . . ."

"Yes?"

Proudly she lifted her head and proudly she looked X. Beidler right in the eye. "When Opal Hevener was killed, John Slocum was in my bed. With me."

7

Slocum couldn't get enough water. Lord, what a thirst! He drank glass after glass. His throat muscles worked fine, denying the weight he still felt around his neck from the rope. The ghost rope. He thought, *I'll feel the real thing one day,* and said, "Pass me that dipper again, Lucia. I'm thirsty as a mule skinner on the Mohave."

Cool, fresh and sweet. MacPherson had an ironic glint in his eye. He knew. The manager savored his own snifter of brandy and shifted his wooden leg on the fender of the big wood stove. The roar of the fire was a little louder than the wail of the wind outdoors. Though Slocum was trying not to show it, the cold was in his bones, and he warmed his hands over the stove and poured water into his dehydrated tissues. "Damn," he said. He opened his mouth so his teeth wouldn't chatter.

Lucia watched the tall, rangy man with a slightly possessive smile. She had a cup of tea cupped in her fingers. She had plenty to ask Slocum but nothing that couldn't wait.

The manager was still angry at the men who hadn't obeyed him in his own mill. Good men, most of them. They were hard workers who'd put in a hard day for a day's pay. But obedience stopped when the shift whistle blew. It wasn't like England, where an employer could count on a doff of the cap no matter where he met his workers, day or night. MacPherson was too canny to retaliate against his men. But he'd be very cranky and irritable the next few days so the miners' insubordination didn't leak over into working hours.

MacPherson wondered about Slocum. Though he was fond of him, the manager wasn't pleased by Lucia's astonishing admission. Tongues would wag. Given the stern code that governed small towns out West, Lucia would be branded a tramp—or worse. The manager thought Lucia had overstayed her welcome. She'd be getting more than her share of sneers and snubs in Blue Rock, and it'd be worse because she had been a fine lady. Well, MacPherson would be writing London tomorrow anyway. Perhaps the memory of her crime had faded. Perhaps she could go home. If Slocum was willing, she could ride to Fort Bozeman with . . . Well, time enough for that later.

"Why did Beidler believe me?" Lucia asked. "Why did he accept my word that you were innocent?"

Slocum shot her a glance. She was quite relaxed, rolling her teacup between her palms. Obviously she expected Slocum to say something like, "How could he doubt the word of a lady?" Slocum said, "He didn't." He lifted his glass. "I'll take a little of that brandy now," he said. "I ain't so thirsty anymore."

MacPherson, smiling, poured him a generous tot.

Lucia was miffed. She rose, her body stiff and her

116

lips set. "Then why did he let you go? He did want to hang you, or was I mistaken?"

"He wouldn't have minded hanging me, no. He's hung a few men and it's like a habit with him. Show that man a rope and he can't help thinking how it'd look around somebody's neck. But Beidler didn't think I killed Opal. He knows men a little better'n that. He was in the mood to hang me, all right, but you gave him a reasonable doubt."

"Oh, come, come," MacPherson objected, "aren't you being a little harsh? After all, he is a law officer. He is trying to rid us of those murderous road agents."

"He never showed me no badge," Slocum remarked dryly. "And I just can't think kindly of a man who keeps invitin' me to dance at the end of a rope."

"Who, then? Who did kill Opal? Who'd murder a girl like that?"

"George Ives. Or the sheriff."

"Oh, come now," Lucia protested. "You can't mean that."

Slocum shrugged. He was carrying a few bruises on his face, one eye was all puffed up and his knuckles were cut to hell.

MacPherson chuckled. "It must have been some fight. I wish I'd seen it. Like a falling out between circus acrobats, what? Some of my miners aren't going to be much use tomorrow."

Slocum shrugged again. "Nobody asked them to come to the party. They could have stayed home in bed."

"I suppose it's a good thing you weren't carrying a sidearm," MacPherson mused. "It could have turned into a real bloodbath."

"For Opal it was," Slocum reminded him.

"Do you own a revolver?" MacPherson had something on his mind.

"Nope."

The manager limped over to a tall walnut cabinet with brass straps. He inserted a small key in the lock and removed a heavy rectangular box. The box was the deep rich purple of old mahogany and it was lined with fitted blue velvet. In velvet compartments were two London Colts. An ornate powder horn, percussion caps and bullet mold each had a smaller compartment of its own. MacPherson checked the cylinder before handing Slocum one of the Colts, butt first.

Slocum checked for himself, anyway. It never did to let another man's eyes do your seeing.

"It's quite empty," Lucia remarked. "Loaded guns in the house are a hazard."

"Guns are always a hazard," Slocum replied. "And they ain't no damn good without bullets in them."

The grips were carved ivory—some sort of helmeted figure on one grip and crossed banners on the other. A little fancy for Slocum's taste, but the balance was fine and the hammer action was slick and one of Colonel Colt's workmen had put a little of himself into this particular iron.

"Nice," Slocum said, handing it back.

MacPherson didn't want to take it. "It's yours to use," he said. "I expect you know how."

" 'Deed I do." Slocum slipped it back into its fitted compartment. "It's a nice gun. Hickok used to claim a man could get off a first shot with a Colt percussion faster than any other pistol made. They're kind of delicate. Nice thing about the Colt Army: You can carry it around for six months and pound fence staples with it, and unless you've soaked it under water, it's gonna fire."

"You need a revolver, Slocum," MacPherson said. "Ever since you arrived in Blue Rock, you've been getting into the sort of trouble a man usually has to shoot his way out of. You attract trouble like honey catches flies, and without a gun, you won't be around much longer."

Slocum set his boots on the stove. He told them the story of the colonel and his promise. He owed them that much, anyway.

Though she listened quietly enough while Slocum told of the former CSA colonel-turned-banker and his forced vow to put away his guns for a year, Lucia was getting angrier by the moment. Slocum finished his tale by saying, ruefully, "It's been all right, I suppose, but it's making me into one hell of a fighter. By the time I can carry a gun again, my hands will be too swollen up to use it."

"But that's insane," Lucia blurted. She got up and paced back and forth like she was addressing a crowd. "A man like you without a gun? Your damn colonel was trying to kill you, don't you understand that?"

"Well, ma'am," Slocum drawled, "I guess he figured he had the right."

"She's right, you know," MacPherson said, seriously. "A man like you without a gun—how do you expect to last through the year?"

Slocum grinned. "Mother wit," he said.

Walker's Saloon was damn cold. Walker was sullen. It was late and the player piano had played "Tenting Tonight on the Old Campground" at least six times in a row. Jim Thiel guessed it was stuck.

When the disgruntled miners finally tramped out of the mill, Beidler ordered them to carry the girl's body down to the Britannia office, where it'd rest until they dynamited a hole for it in the frozen earth. The tarp they rolled her in was a good foot or two short. A couple of men got pretty liberally smeared with Opal Hevener's blood. That didn't noticeably improve their tempers.

Walker's was closed, but, by God, after this night's dirty business, they all wanted a drink, and since Walker slept upstairs, it was easy to wake him by beating on the door until the sleepy bartender stumbled downstairs in his nightshirt to let them in. He didn't want to open up, but a couple of angry men convinced him that he'd damn well better or they'd break the door down, and drinks would be on the house until all the booze was gone. Walker saw reason and opened the door. He got behind the bar. He said, not very graciously, "What'll you have, suckers?"

What they wanted was rye whiskey. What they got was trade whiskey. A man didn't want to sip it, but it did warm the belly and blot out the memories of the night.

A couple of men tried to start up a game of stud, but even the gambling types weren't really in the mood and the game fizzled out. Most of them stood at the bar, and when they finished one drink, they started another. Nobody was talking much except George Ives and the sheriff. They'd happened by to see what all the noise was about.

Tersely, somebody told of the night's events. Tersely, someone cursed X. Beidler for believing Lucia MacPherson.

One said, "He killed that damn poor girl sure as I'm standin' here, and the squarehead turns him loose on that female's say-so. And then"—his voice became an angry squeak—"he orders us to carry the bloody mess down to the company office, and it leaked all over my good shirt." He glared at the stains on his sleeve.

The sheriff was jovial. "You boys should have notified me," he said. "Me or George. I said all along we should hang that jasper Slocum. Now he's gone and killed George's lady friend."

George Ives was still gray in the face from Slocum's kick. Maybe that's the reason he was hitting the booze so hard. "So, she's dead," he said to nobody in particular. "Unfaithful cunt. Well, it serves her right. She takes up with a killer like Slocum and he kills her. She should have known better."

Thiel was leaning against the bar, surveying the scene. He wasn't drunk and he intended staying that way. Two other miners would be traveling with him in the morning: the buck-toothed kid and an old Italian named Gus. They were hitting the sauce pretty hard, and one of the party would need to have a clear head for the journey.

When Sheriff Hammer came over for a refill, Thiel remarked casually, "Slocum said Georgie did it. Or you and Georgie. He said he didn't have anything to do with it."

Sheriff Hammer flashed him a blinding smile so quick that Thiel almost missed the rage in his eyes. He clapped Thiel on the back. "Man'll say any damn-fool thing when he's got a rope around his neck," he said. "Let me buy you a drink."

"No thanks."

The sheriff's eyebrows rose to half-mast. "You sayin' you won't drink with me? You sayin' you believe that son of a bitch?"

Jim Thiel, being a peaceable man, said, "No, no. No offense. I'm leavin' tomorrow for Fort Bozeman and I want to keep a clear head."

The sheriff grinned at him and said, "Drink it, Jim. How come you never told me you was leavin'? Hell, you know I wouldn't want to wake up tomorrow and find you gone and have to learn about it from the bunch of drunks in here. Fort Bozeman, eh?"

Thiel accepted the drink. "Yes," he said.

"Well, I hope you found what you were lookin' for here in Blue Rock."

The sheriff was sort of asking a question without actually asking it, and Jim answered, a little too quick, "No, Sheriff Hammer, I didn't have any luck here at all. Hell, it was all I could do to hang onto my grub-stake. I never struck it rich."

The sheriff winked at him before he said, way too loud for Thiel's taste, loud enough so his voice carried to every man in the room, "Of course you didn't strike it rich, Jim. Hell, a man who works as hard as you do pannin', sluicin' all day long and, in the summer, half the night, that's the kind of man who never strikes it rich. It's the lazy bastards like me who get rich—like that man who found the Comstock lode when his damn mule scraped a rock over and it turned out to be pure gold. Ain't that true? No way a hard worker like you is gonna get rich."

Thiel had a little over $500 in dust hidden under an old washpot outside his cabin. He'd be carrying that much tomorrow. "I guess that's true," he said, laughing, trying to turn a non-joke into a joke and trying to ignore George Ives's eyes on him and his steady smile. "I guess that's damn true. The workin' man never gets rich, ain't that true, sheriff? Ain't that true?"

And Sheriff Hammer laughed with him, haw, haw, haw, but nobody else was laughing, not even Thiel's two partners.

"I'll have company on the trail," Thiel said, trying to sound casual. "Yes, a couple good boys to ride alongside me."

The sheriff's blinding smile. "Oh, yeah? That's fine, Jim. Man can't have too many trail partners in times like these. Who?"

For some reason, Jim Thiel wanted to answer the sheriff's question with a lie. He wanted to say, "John Slocum'll be riding with me." But instead he pointed wordlessly at the kid and Gus, both of whom were drowning their sorrows.

And the sheriff looked at the two of them and said, "Fine men, Jim. They'll do to ride the river with. Have another drink."

Jim Thiel didn't want this drink, either, but hell, maybe the sheriff was just being friendly. Maybe the sheriff meant what he said. Maybe the sheriff was just wishing him well. Jim took another drink, and when the sheriff offered to clink glasses—a toast in honor of whatever understanding they'd reached—Jim clinked glasses with him, though what he really wanted to do was throw the glass in the sheriff's face and start yelling for help.

The sheriff gave him one last grin before he turned to bellow at Walker, "Walker! What's the matter with that damn machine of yours? It only know one tune?"

"Tenting tonight, tenting tonight, tenting tonight on the old campground . . ."

"I can't change rolls when it's cold," Walker explained. "The wax gets brittle. If you try and get a cylinder out, you wreck it for good."

"Well, hell," the sheriff said. "I don't like that damn tune, anyway." He raised his voice. "Anybody in here like this damn tune?"

Men found places to look. Some got real interested in the dregs of their drinks. Others peered intently at the wet rings on the bar.

"No?" the sheriff asked again. "You sure? I'd sure hate to turn any of you gents against me on the eve of the election, because I sure do enjoy being your sheriff and I intend to keep the job for another year." Suddenly he spun back to peer at Thiel. "How about it, Thiel? You gonna vote for me?"

"I won't be in Blue Rock tomorrow afternoon," Thiel said, begging the question.

"So you won't. So you won't. Well, then," the sheriff said, laughing, "no sense inquirin' after your musical tastes, is there?" He'd made another joke, so Thiel dutifully laughed.

Walker said, "Wait a damn moment," but before he was out from behind the bar, George Ives was standing in front of him, saying, "I think you wanted to buy me a drink." And while Walker poured George's drink with trembling hands, Sheriff Hammer ripped the wax cylinder out of the player piano. It squalled to a halt. The sheriff went through the neat chest of piano rolls, pulling them out and discarding them one after another. "Can't find what I want," he said, and tossed one aside. "Can't find what I want, just can't find it." And another roll smashed on the floor. When the whole collection of music rolls was strewn around his feet, he turned to Walker. "Say," he said mildly, "I was sure you had it."

Walker's strangled voice: "What?"

Sheriff Hammer's languid smile. " 'Tenting Tonight on the Old Campground.' It's my favorite."

"Do you really think Sheriff Hammer had a hand in Opal's death?" Lucia asked.

"Uh-huh," Slocum said.

Pharoah MacPherson was sitting at his desk writing a letter. It must have been a difficult letter for him to write, because from time to time he'd swear, tear up the draft and carefully begin again.

Lucia was sitting a little too close to Slocum—or not quite close enough, depending on how you looked at it. She wanted to talk about poor Opal, but Slocum had already put his memories of the girl aside to lay with the other sad memories he had, for examination and regrets when he was alone beside some lonely campfire. No sense worrying about the dead. It didn't bring them back.

But Lucia kept badgering him. "Well, if you think the sheriff and George Ives are guilty of murder, what are you going to do about it?"

"Maybe I'll go on a hunger strike," Slocum said. "That'll change things."

Lucia flushed. She snapped, "There are different tactics for different situations, Mr. Slocum. The hunger strike—"

"Didn't get you the vote. Not so far as I've heard."

"You are so superior. You are so damn superior. You can sit and make judgments on anything, except in the one case, the single case where there's something for you to do, you sit on your . . . hands!"

Slocum smiled. He said, "Oh, I suppose I'll do something about those two. I just ain't in any rip-roaring hurry."

"That's fine. I thought Opal meant something to you. I thought you cared about her."

"I did."

"Well, what are you going to do about it? How are you going to avenge her?"

"Lucia," Slocum said, "an old Comanche once told me something about revenge. He said: 'Revenge is a dish that's best served cold.' " And when he spoke, something cold came into his eyes, and though his voice didn't change from its idle bantering tone, Lucia knew the matter was decided.

MacPherson rose from his desk. "Here," he said to Slocum. "I received this communication this morning. You'd better read it." MacPherson handed a second letter, his reply, to Lucia.

> To: The Honorable P. MacPherson
>   Mine Manager, Britannia Mine
>
> Dear Pharoah,
>   As you know, June 17 is the date of Her Majesty's Silver Jubilee. The commemoration will take place at Westminster, but, additionally, many English firms will take space at the Pavilion, where they hope to demonstrate processes, goods and innovations. It should be quite a show. The directors have asked me to plan an exhibit for Megathorp Mining, Ltd., and I can think of nothing more unusual to offer than the gold nugget mentioned in your report. Such a find will impress every Englishman with the promise of our firm. The press will certainly be excited. And since, at present, Megathorp is seeking concessions on the Transvaal, every bit of interest we can create will be to our advantage. Therefore, I am requesting that you ship the nugget to London to arrive before June 17. (And, Pharoah, is the damn thing really as big as you say it is?)
>
>   Yours,
>   JAMES STOCKWELL
>   Director, Megathorp Mining, Ltd.

Slocum read the letter and whistled soundlessly. He handed it back. "Now, ain't that a hell of a note," he said.

"Arrived just today. I've been thinking about it most of the afternoon. Slocum," MacPherson said enthusi-

125

astically, "you have no idea what a glorious occasion this is going to be. The Jubilee of England's greatest ruler. The Blue Rock nugget on prominent display. I must confess my excitement."

"Uh-huh. How you gonna get it there?"

MacPherson started to reply, but Lucia interrupted him. "Whose damn idea was this?" she asked, waving MacPherson's reply. "Who thinks I, quote, 'should return, perhaps, to English soil, where her prospects are better'?"

MacPherson smiled thinly. "One doesn't meet too many appropriate suitors here in Blue Rock, Montana," he said.

"So? I never went around looking for appropriate suitors when I was in England. What makes you think, Uncle dear, that I'll be more interested now?"

"You can't stay here," MacPherson snapped. "Lucia, I'm sorry. No decent person in Blue Rock will associate with you since you've admitted to your affair with Slocum, and you certainly aren't thinking of marrying him."

"I've had no affair, and why not?"

MacPherson was confused. "Then why did you say—"

"Because the damn fool is innocent. Isn't that reason enough?"

"Are you informing me that you and he are to be married?" MacPherson was totally lost. Nothing he said was going to be right.

"She ain't been asked," Slocum said. He was enjoying himself.

"Uncle, I will do as I choose, with whom I choose and where I choose. It is no concern of yours." Her aristocratic face was a frozen mask.

MacPherson sighed. "Yes, I suppose you will. But not in Blue Rock. I don't care where you go after you reach Fort Bozeman. I'd hope it was London. I shan't allow you to remain here."

Lucia bit her lip, but MacPherson was right and

she knew it, and she had no more liking for slurs and leers than he did.

His eyes softened. "It's for your own good," he said.

"I'll be the judge of that," she snapped. She may have surrendered, but she wasn't going to beg.

MacPherson turned to Slocum. "I want you to escort her," he said. "Her and the gold."

Slocum grinned. "Ain't that kind of like asking the fox to guard the chicken house?"

"Not if you give me your word."

"Last time I gave my word, it got me in a hell of a bind. Why don't you use twenty or thirty of your miners? Or bring gunmen up from Fort Bozeman? I saw two or three boys down there that used to be regulators for the Cattlemen's Association. They ain't exactly gentlemen, but they'd get your gold through." Slocum smiled. "Of course, you'd want to have somebody at the other end expecting it."

MacPherson waved away the suggestion. "No time," he said. "From here to Bozeman is three days. From the fort to the railhead at the Platte, another week— two weeks in this weather. Then to New York and ultimately London. The gold must leave Blue Rock by the day after tomorrow. When we arrive at Fort Bozeman, you can hire some reliable men to escort us to the railhead."

"Us?" Slocum took a long, slow sip of brandy. He wasn't going to like what he was going to hear.

Impatiently, MacPherson barked, "Figure it yourself, man. There are exactly four people in Blue Rock I trust. X. Beidler is one and the other three are in this room. Lucia has to leave, anyway. Under our protection, it shouldn't be dangerous for her."

" 'Our'? I'm a market hunter, MacPherson. I've sworn not to shoot another man. Tomorrow I'm going back into the mountains after elk."

MacPherson was pacing. Back and forth. Back and forth. "How many men in Blue Rock know of your vow?"

"I ain't told nobody except you two. But if the road agents come at us, I won't do no good. I ain't got no more teeth than a teddy bear."

MacPherson smacked his fist into the palm of his hand. "But that's the beauty of it, don't you see? The road agents don't know you can't shoot back. They won't want to tangle with you." He surveyed Slocum critically. "You have the look of a dangerous man."

"When they start shooting, I'll just tell them how dangerous I am. Maybe they'll run away," Slocum said bitterly.

MacPherson strode to his desk and opened the small safe. Slocum was trying to catch Lucia's eye, but she was furious at her uncle and, by extension, at all men and wouldn't meet his gaze. MacPherson returned with a sheaf of greenbacks. He pushed them at Slocum. "One thousand dollars, Mr. Slocum. Once we reach Fort Bozeman, there'll be another thousand to get the gold nugget and my niece to New York."

The money could mean a lot. Slocum never liked being poor. He wouldn't mind waiting in the relatively civilized East until his word ran out. "No," he said. "I'd get you killed."

MacPherson struggled to hide his disappointment. The bills drooped in his hand like an embarrassment. He coughed. "Very well. Then I shall accompany Lucia. I am a trained marksman, and Lucia can shoot as well as most men."

Lucia had a hint of steel in her voice. "We'll take the nugget ourselves. It will make a lovely story to tell in polite circles once I reach London."

You ain't ever gonna reach London, Slocum thought. *Not one chance in a thousand.* His brandy tasted horrible. He made a face. "If you're damn fool enough to go," he said, "I'm damn fool enough to go with you."

It was only three hours till sunrise. Jim Thiel nursed his drink and waited. His two partners had already

128

stumbled off to gather all their belongings.

"We'll get a good start first thing in the morning," the kid had said, all smiles.

Life looks pretty good at 20, Thiel had thought, but he'd said, "Sure, kid. Early start. Quick trip."

No sense bothering them with his fears. One way or another, they'd still want to go. The kid was so anxious to get moving he could taste it, and Gus, the Italian, had promised to meet his brother at the fort. He wouldn't want to wait, either. Still, Thiel wished that Gus could speak better English. If only he'd been able to share his worries, they wouldn't have seemed so ominous.

Thiel was already packed up. All he had to do was retrieve his poke, saddle his horse and toss his possibles behind the saddle. That was one of his faults: He worried about every little thing that might go wrong. Consequently, he was often half a day ahead of himself.

Most of the other miners were gone. A few, who'd put away too much of Walker's whiskey, were snoring among the cases and mops in the back room. Three others were sitting up over a bottle. Each wanted his exact share every time they refilled glasses. They eyed one another suspiciously, drunk as skunks, and didn't say much except, "Al, it's your turn to pour. You make it fair, hear?"

Walker was half asleep on a stool behind the bar. Infrequently, he'd open one rheumy eye to see that nobody was setting fire to the place. Sometimes he'd snore and wake himself up.

The sheriff and George Ives sat in the corner having a quiet argument. They kept their voices low and glanced around pretty often. Thiel overheard only bits of it.

George slammed his glass down and said, "I'll be damned if I let him get away with it. He's my business. Nobody . . ."

Ives hushed when Sheriff Hammer put his hand on his arm and then the two of them turned as one and

129

saw Thiel watching them. Sheriff Hammer put up one big finger and, smiling, tut, tut, tutted with it. "Little pitchers have big ears," he said, just loud enough so that Walker opened one eye for a second. Ives wasn't smiling. He yanked his arm away from the sheriff's hand and whispered fiercely and the sheriff nodded, but his eyes never left Thiel's face and his smile stayed like it was painted there.

Thiel looked away. He looked at Walker. He looked at the three drunks. He looked at the back bar mirror. He counted three bullet holes in the mirror, but they were near the edge and didn't spoil the reflection. He didn't look at the part of the mirror that reflected George and the sheriff. His ears were cocked and he heard the sheriff say, "We'll take care of him later. Afterward. No sense letting personal matters get in the way of business."

For some reason, Thiel felt a cold chill down his spine. When he heard the footsteps coming up behind him, the chill turned to ice. He jerked around and saw Sheriff Hammer's big, bland, smiling face. The sheriff stood easily, like a man who already has everything he wants.

"You sure aren't hittin' it very hard tonight, Jim," he said. "Here, let me buy you a bottle. Walker!"

Walker's eyes looked like bloodshot lanterns. When he saw who wanted him, he came but not without muttering. Sheriff Hammer flipped a couple of silver cartwheels into the sawdust behind the bar. "You know, Walker, you're a lousy barkeep. One night somethin' is gonna happen to you and somebody else'll set up and we'll all be much, much happier."

The sheriff pushed the bottle in front of Thiel and said, "Now, this is my farewell present to you, Jim. My little way of sayin' good-by. I believe you ought to drink it here, tonight. I get terrible upset when someone won't shake my hand or drink my booze. He stuck out his hand. Numbly Thiel took it. He felt like a child entrusting his hand to his daddy. "Good." The sheriff smiled. "You know, Jim, you're a helluva fellow. Just a helluva fellow. I'm tuckered. I'm gonna get some shut-eye. But George, he's one of those insomniacs. He can't sleep worth a damn. He says he doesn't want to drink with you because you don't like him. You do like Georgie, don't you?" The sheriff's face was merely curious.

"I don't give a damn for him," Thiel said thickly.

The sheriff produced another of his marvelous smiles." You know, I don't blame you a bit." He lowered his voice to a whisper. "Sometimes George Ives is a terrible pain in the ass." He laughed. "You just drink up. And you think well of me while you're doin' it. George'll be right here—in case you get lonely."

Pharoah MacPherson was the sort of man who was happiest when working on a blueprint or a technical problem. The two men were bent over his desk, making drawings for the gold sled. It would need to be narrow to negotiate the Blue Rock Trail and high off the runners so it wouldn't drag in heavy snow. They thought a team of four Morgans could draw it, with MacPherson at the reins, Lucia alongside the leader and John Slocum as scout.

"Maybe you can't shoot a man," MacPherson said, "but if you see anyone, give them a few near misses. These road agents are a cowardly bunch and won't care for bullets whizzing by."

Slocum hoped that was true.

"Lucia and I will be armed, and I assure you: Neither of us is afraid."

"I wish you were," Slocum said.

While the men made their plans, Lucia was curled up on the chaise with a cup of tea. Once she smiled at Slocum, and Slocum was glad he had to pay attention to MacPherson's blueprint. It was getting a little warm in there.

They planned to anchor the cargo with ringbolts,

and MacPherson promised some heavy chains from the Britannia's shop to lash it. When he was finally satisfied, he folded the blueprint and slipped it into his pocket. "I'll get my foreman on this first thing in the morning," he said.

"I'll want to pick the horses," Slocum said.

"There are a dozen good Morgans at the mine. In the spring we'll pull our ore wagons with them, but right now they're pretty fat and sassy."

"We'll need provisions: food, ammunition, spare harness, oats for the horses, shovels and picks . . ."

"Well, we've got those, certainly, but whatever for?"

"Avalanches. This time of year we might spend a couple days digging our way through. And we'll need some dynamite in case we have to blast."

MacPherson scribbled down Slocum's needs and said, "Well, that seems to be the lot. I'm to bed. Tomorrow will be a long day." With real fondness in his eyes, he wished Lucia good night.

"Good night, Uncle."

MacPherson stopped at the bottom of the stairs, as if undecided, and turned to glance at Slocum. He opened his mouth, thought better of it, shook his head and said, "None of my business, I suppose," before he left them there together.

The house creaked and groaned in the wind. Slocum took out the makings of a smoke. The scratch of his match sounded very loud.

Lucia walked up behind him and started kneading his neck. Softly she said, "You're very loose, John."

"Loose as a goose." He tossed his cigarette into the fire, rose and met her lips.

Her mouth was open, seeking.

He busied himself with the ties of her simple gray dress. Her fingers hurried over the buttons of his shirt. Impatiently, she tugged at his pants. She broke from the kiss long enough to say, "Oh, damn! Why is this always so awkward!"

"Easy now," Slocum said. "Slow down." Like he was gentling a skittish horse.

She doused the lantern and stood before him, dress loosened, her fine eyes shining. "John," she said. "I . . . I . . ."

"Hush," he said.

He slipped her dress over her shoulders and it dropped, whispering, to the floor. She stepped out of the slick pile of cloth.

Slocum stared at Lucia's high breasts, long neck, long arms and the surprising swell of her rich hips and the neat triangle tucked below. He could smell the woman of her.

Just as frankly, she admired his body. Her hand brushed his cock.

"Easy now," Slocum said again, but this time he was gentling himself, not her.

Hand in hand, they walked to the chaise.

They spent a very long time exploring each other, every texture of skin, every silkiness, every prolonged gasp. And when he pushed into her, they were both mindless, tormented almost beyond relief, but it came, it came, and Slocum heard, in that last instant, that Lucia was quietly, joyfully humming.

When dawn finally arrived, Walker was snoring behind the bar. The sole remaining drunk was staring at the quarter-inch of rotgut remaining in his bottle, wondering if he still had the coordination to pour the booze into his glass and transport the glass to his mouth. He just didn't know.

George Ives was turning over greasy cards in a boring game of solitaire. *Slap, slap, slap.*

Jim Thiel was drunk and he had to be sober, though he couldn't remember why.

About an hour after Sheriff Hammer left, he got up and, abandoning the nearly full bottle, headed for the door. He almost made it, too, but George Ives's high whine stopped him. "Sheriff said you was to drink up all that whiskey," Ives said. "Said he'd be real offended if you didn't. Said I was to tell you that." George yawned and shuffled the cards. "Sheriff said if you don't let him show his"—he groped for the right word—"friendship, yeah, that's it, he'd take it out on me."

Thiel was tired and a little loaded, and George wasn't half Sheriff Hammer's size. "So fucking what?" Thiel snarled.

George turned his card and stared at it. He shook his head and got to his feet. His hand hung right by his gun butt. "Jim Thiel," he said, "I think you're a nice enough fellow for a Cornishman. I'd hate like hell to kill you."

So. Message received.

Thiel sat back down and drank the whiskey, trying not to get drunk, trying to let enough time pass between drinks so he could keep his wits about him. After a couple of hours, he was doing okay. He'd finished a third of the bottle and was in fairly good shape. *I'm a big man,* he thought. *I can drink a lot of this stuff before it starts to hurt me.* He thought he was going to get away free.

He decided to wait until George was engrossed in his solitaire game and then he'd pour some of the bottle into the sawdust. The first time George's eyes were focused on the cards, Thiel poured a couple of drinks away.

George sighed, stood up and walked over to him. "Jesus Christ, Thiel—you *want* to die?" He pulled his pistol and shoved it against Thiel's throat. He was pushing hard, and from the look on his face, he was enjoying it, too.

Thiel was choking but didn't dare raise his hands. With his free hand, George unstrapped Thiel's holster flap and pulled out the old Walker Colt, then backed off to examine the gun.

"Jesus H. Christ"—he whistled—"I never thought to see the day one of these damn things turned up in

Blue Rock." George extracted the bullets one by one and dropped them on the floor before he handed the heavy six-gun back to Thiel. He said, "What a piece of junk," and poured Thiel a brimming drink of whiskey. "It ain't safe for you to be carrying a loaded gun," he explained. "Not when you're drinkin' so heavy."

When the first dim light sneaked in through the windows, George checked his watch and yawned. He stacked the deck of cards neatly in the middle of the poker table. When he came over to Thiel, he hefted the empty bottle and said, "Good. The sheriff'll be happy you liked his present." Then, surprisingly, he reached over and patted the big drunk miner's cheek and smiled at him. A real smile. "Your friends'll be coming to get you soon," he said. "And don't you worry. Hell, you're so drunk you won't feel a thing."

8

If MacPherson had any comments to make the next morning, he didn't make them. Slocum had one eye open when the mine manager tiptoed down the stairs, peered at the rumpled, tangled lovers, drew on his boots and closed the door softly behind him.

Slocum lay on the narrow chaise, with the warmth of Lucia's long, lovely body pressed against him and her head on his arm. When he brushed the touseled hair back from her face, she murmured "Wha?" without waking. John Slocum lay under the quilts and blankets and was happy. Drowsy and happy. He listened to the sounds of MacPherson's miners starting their day's work. He heard the clatter of the Britannia's cages, the whine of ropes over the sheaves at the top of the headframe, the calls of the men, one to another. He felt pretty good, lying warm beside a beautiful woman.

It was one of the rewards for living life at a breakneck pace. Slocum never thought he'd grow old. It never occurred to him that he might. He had nothing squirreled away for a time when his strength failed him and his reflexes slowed. He owned no land, no bank accounts, no investments. His family was dead or scattered to the four winds. He had a few friends and a few more enemies. He never knew, from month to month, whether he'd be eating caviar in a fine Denver restaurant or cold beans out of the can. Now and again, on some lonely trail at night, with the cold wind blowing, he'd **ride** by a nester's soddy. He'd look at the bright windows and hear the sounds of a family inside and feel—just about the way one would expect him to feel.

Because it was so rare to lie in bed with a good woman while other men went about doing the business of the world, it was especially fine. In Slocum's dangerous life, such moments were few and far between, so he valued them and made them last.

When he finally got up, he was careful not to wake the woman. On the brink of consciousness, she murmured something again, but when he stroked her long neck, she eased back into slumber.

The fire had died back, but it was still warm in the house, and all the sunlight a man could want was streaming through the windows. Slocum stretched, got into his duds and stepped out onto the front porch with a basin of wash water. The porch was above the mine yard. The miners were wrestling timbers toward the shaft head and the foreman was calling at them to get the lead out. Slocum recognized one or two men from the night before. They moved slower and more clumsily than the rest. Slocum smiled. He was glad their vigilante excursion had cost them something.

The morning was warm, the snow was melting, and Blue Rock Creek was running swollen, brown and loud. It felt like a chinook, one of the rare warm winds of winter that make a man hope for spring. By nightfall it'd lock up again, the melted snow would turn to ice and winter would be just as treacherous as before, but now, this morning, the day was as lovely as a young girl and as full of promise.

136

With a tremendous squeal, the steam engine lifted the 20-ton stamp. Slocum heard men cursing as they swabbed the remains of Opal Hevener into mop buckets. Then the cam swung over, the ore tumbled onto the stamp table and the mill was running again: *whump, hiss, whump, hiss, whump, hiss.*

The back of the stove still held enough heat to cook. Slocum sliced some slabs off a piece of bacon and set his frying pan to sizzling. While the bacon fried, he padded quietly into the back of the house to check out the gold he'd be hauling tomorrow.

When he pulled back the tarp, the damn thing glowed like a million wedding rings; the brilliant white strip of quartz was dull by comparison. It made Slocum want to laugh. Enough money for any man for his lifetime tied up in this big, terribly heavy hunk of rock. It glowed like a faintly malevolent alien idol. Slocum walked around it. It glowed on the back side, too. Slocum scratched his head and smiled. When he put his hand on the nugget, it was ice cold. He patted it like he'd pat a big, slightly dim-witted dog. He shook his head. They'd move it, all right. They'd get it all the way to London. But he'd never seen anything so valuable that looked so silly.

"John?" Lucia called.

Slocum went back to the front and checked his bacon. It smelled real good. He pushed the bacon aside and cracked eggs into the pan.

Lucia drowsily slipped into her robe. She moved with the grace and naked beauty of a sleepy lioness.

Slocum turned the eggs. "Come and get it before I throw it out." He poured two cups of steaming black coffee and they sat down, and when Lucia felt Slocum's eyes on her, she dropped her eyes to her plate and blushed.

"I heard you moving around in back," she said. "Will it be dangerous moving the nugget?"

"Yep. There'll be a few people around who wouldn't mind stealing it."

"How will we protect it?"

"Well"—Slocum smiled—"suppose we cross that bridge when we come to it."

When he finished with his meal, he gathered his rifles, spread out some newspapers and unpacked his tools: gun oil, gun grease, hones and small screwdrivers. He disassembled each gun, oiled it and scrupulously wiped the excess oil off the slick metal parts. He tried the actions and honed the sear of the Colt revolving rifle.

While he worked over the guns, Lucia watched him. Finally she said, "When we women get the vote, we'll outlaw those damnable things." She spoke so quietly Slocum barely heard her. He was working the hammer on the Sharps.

"Don't tell too many men about that," Slocum advised, "or you never will get the vote."

"Do you know how tired women are of having their men go off and come back all shot up, to be invalids for the rest of their lives?"

"I bet invalids don't care for it, either." Slocum peered through the bore of the Sharps, checking for powder flecks that could pit the rifling.

Lucia was determined to be real serious. Slocum thought it might be her way of recovering from their lovemaking.

"John, do you think women should have the vote?"

He smiled at her—his most infuriating smile—and said, "Don't give a damn. I got the vote and it never did me much good. Go around voting all the time and all you do is encourage the senators and governors and them boys. It's like you gave 'em a license for their foolishness."

Lucia would not be put off by his mockery. "Mr. Slocum, I speak French, Latin, a little German. I am versed in history and the arts. I can ride a horse with any man and shoot better than most. I can, and have, entertained at dinner parties for nobility. Yet the most

138.

ignorant of my father's miners has the vote and I haven't."

"Sure," Slocum said. "It's a real nice mornin'. Maybe after you're done wolfin' that grub, we can take a stroll."

"Damn you," she snapped.

But Slocum gave her one of his best grins and she chuckled. "Speakin' of the vote," Slocum asked, "how did that horse's ass ever get himself elected sheriff?"

"You'll see this afternoon," she said.

As she spoke, Slocum watched the miners through the window. A crew of men was swarming all over a wooden platform that was beginning to resemble a sled. From where he sat, they were making a good job of it.

Blue Rock's electoral system was practical and odd. Once a year—today, in fact—the miners gathered and cast their ballots. Naturally, they nominated a fair crowd of men—10 or 15, anyway. Anyone with three votes was a legitimate nominee. Most of the nominees withdrew before the runoff in the Britannia's corral. The men who wanted to be sheriff stood in that corral and, at a signal, commenced the donnybrook. No holds barred and the last man standing was the new sheriff.

"So," Lucia concluded, "Blue Rock elects its toughest, most brutal citizen to be its sheriff. It isn't right."

"No," Slocum agreed. "It probably isn't. But Sheriff Hammer isn't the most powerful man in Blue Rock; your uncle is. Who elected him? His money?"

Slocum might have said more, but Lucia clobbered him with a pillow—*whoomp*—and the air was white with feathers. Soon they were both at it, silly as two kids, belting each other. Roaring with laughter, neither of them heard the door open, and when Slocum turned to face the draft and a bewildered Pharoah MacPherson, Lucia got in one last shot—*whoomp!*

Pharoah was more upset at his niece's lovemaking than he dared let on. Maybe he didn't think Slocum was good enough for her; maybe he was angry there'd be no marriage. He stood in the doorway, dressed in his work clothes. His hands were grimy with oil. His mouth was set in disapproval. He said, "Quite a mess you've created here," and marched into the back of the house. Lucia made a funny face at Slocum, and Slocum gritted his teeth to keep from laughing.

MacPherson returned with a broom. The two lovers watched as he cleaned up the debris. He cleaned very noisily. When MacPherson swept close to the chaise, Slocum lifted his feet. "Sled's almost ready?" Slocum asked.

"Yes."

"Anybody been up the trail from Fort Bozeman?"

"No."

"Beidler figure who killed Opal?"

"No. You can put your feet down now."

MacPherson was too proud to admit what was bothering him. Since Lucia was an independent woman, quite beyond his control, and he couldn't influence or change things in any important way, he became angrier.

With the manager feeling like this, Slocum thought, it was going to be a long, long trip to Fort Bozeman. Still, there wasn't much he could say about it.

Lucia resolved the difficulty. She said, in her sweetest voice, "Yes, uncle. He did it to me. He went and stuck his dirty thing in me. And you know what? I liked it." Then she produced a smile that lit up her whole face.

MacPherson dropped the broom. He gaped. He turned red. He started for the desk and his London Colt, then stopped because he didn't know whom he'd shoot. And then he laughed and laughed until his face hurt.

Slocum was laughing, too. Lucia reached out and took his hand.

"Damn me, sir. Damn me," MacPherson sputtered. And he put out his hand and John Slocum took it. "I hope you have better luck taming her than I've had," he chuckled. "She's a hellion, that's for certain."

While they ate their lunch, MacPherson filled them in on the gossip about the sheriff's election. Not too many men wanted the job. Fewer wanted it when they got a good look at Sheriff Hammer, who was, he had announced, "running for office in my hobnail boots." A couple of MacPherson's workmen intended to take him on. If nothing else, they had long-standing grudges with the sheriff and the election was a good excuse to get in a few legal licks without getting pistol-whipped by George Ives and thrown into the hoosegow for good measure.

The manager had seen Jim Thiel ride out of town. "He was as drunk as I've seen any man. He has no business riding the trail in his condition. His partners are, well, they're weak reeds, and without Thiel the party is an open invitation to the road agents."

After MacPherson went back to the mine, Lucia was up for a little more lovemaking. Slocum was real tempted, but he had some business to do. "Later," he said. "We've got all the time in the world."

She stamped her foot. "John Slocum, are you going to just walk on out of here?"

"Unless I sprout wings," Slocum drawled as he scooped up his hat.

He slipped through the door just ahead of her coffee cup and a formidable collection of curses. *Never did know a lady who could swear like that,* he reflected cheerfully. *Sure keeps life interesting.*

The sun was glaring off the melting snow, and the street was a mess of snow, slush and mud. A man could sink to his knees in some of the potholes.

Most of Blue Rock was at work and only a few idlers watched the lanky figure as he hopped the puddles, heading downtown. A few of them made remarks about "murderers" and "woman killers," but not so loud that Slocum overheard them.

X. Beidler was standing just behind a crowd of men outside the livery. He was puffing meditatively on his cigar, and when Slocum moved up beside him, he stared straight ahead.

"Mornin'," Slocum said.

Beidler grunted.

Walker was lugging some of the liveryman's belongings out of the livery. He had a wooden table outside and he put the articles out for anyone's inspection. There wasn't much: a shaving mug, a battered New Testament, an Ingersoll watch, a framed photograph of a young black woman, a barlow knife and a set of spectacles in a soft leather case.

"Nobody'll bid much until they bring out the harnesses." He glanced at Slocum. "Hope you're feelin' all right after last night."

Slocum raised his eyebrows. "Didn't think you'd care much one way or the other."

Deadpan, Beidler said, "Sooner or later I'm gonna hang you, John Slocum. I'd hate to see you all nervous and sickly when your day comes."

Slocum was feeling too good to let Beidler walk over his grave. "It's nice to know a man's friends are thinking about him," he said.

Beidler grunted again and the fire went out of his eyes.

Since the liveryman didn't have any living relatives, they were auctioning off his meager belongings to pay the cost of burying him. The bidding was pretty slow. Nobody seemed to care except a tall, cadaverous figure on the edge of the crowd who winced every time an item was knocked down for less than it was worth. When the stag-handled barlow knife brought just 25 cents, he couldn't contain himself. "Walker," he cried, "that knife's worth a dollar if it's worth a dime. How come you letting it go so cheap? You're takin' the bread right out of my mouth. I ain't had a payin' funeral in three damn months. Those damn road agents never leave a penny on their poor, helpless victims." (He became overcome by professional grief.) "And it ain't worthwhile buryin' 'em. This is the first man of property I'll bury all winter. Walker," he wailed, "I got to make a living, too."

"Nobody's keepin' you from biddin', Duggan," Walker observed. "Hell, bid 'em up."

"Now, what in God's name would I do with an-

142

other barlow knife?" the undertaker complained. "I already got a pocket knife."

"So does everybody else," Walker explained reasonably. "That's why it brought only two bits."

Slocum leaned over to Beidler's ear. "George or the sheriff killed Opal Hevener."

Beidler puffed on his cigar. After a while he took it out of his mouth and inspected the ash. "I thought of that," he said.

"You gonna do anything about it?"

"Proof positive, Slocum. I require proof positive." He smiled a self-satisfied smile.

"You ain't exactly investigating at a reckless pace," Slocum noted.

When Walker brought the harnesses out, the bidding grew more animated and the undertaker was rubbing his hands together.

Beidler faced Slocum with his fat face, his fat cigar and his unblinking, pale eyes. "I'm a little like death, Mr. Slocum. I get there. It may take me a while, but I always get there."

Despite himself, Slocum felt a chill. But he smiled and said, "Always did like a man who could tell a good joke, Beidler. That's what all of us need: a little more laughter in our lives." He inclined his head toward the undertaker. "He gonna bury Opal?"

"I have no idea. I lose interest when the flesh gets cold."

"Uh-huh."

The undertaker was leaning against the side of the livery, gumming a toothpick. He was a thin, gangly gent whose wrists stuck out of his sleeves like a plowboy's. He wore a fat gold watch on a silver chain fastened across his middle.

"You gonna bury Opal Hevener?" Slocum asked.

The undertaker made a face. "I guess so." His eyes had the disconcerting habit of wandering around without ever lighting on anything.

"What do you get for it?"

"Two dollars. Two damn dollars. The town gives

143

five dollars to the man who builds the pine box and he's a damn mick." When he snickered, his eyes did light briefly on Slocum's face. Slocum had seen eyes like that on a magpie. "The carpenter will make a little on Opal. The box can be half size." He snickered again. He craned his neck around and stared at the clouds. He examined the earth near Slocum's feet. "Two damn dollars. I got to use dynamite to make a hole, and you think the town pays for the dynamite? No siree!"

"I want you to put up a stone," Slocum said. "I want a little stone over her grave with her name on it: 'Opal Hevener.' "

"Are you kin to the deceased, brother?" the undertaker asked. He got real interested, but his eyes were still flying around like they had a will of their own.

"Nope. How much?"

"Well, I do carry a few monuments. There isn't too much call for stone. Most are satisfied with wooden markers. I do not approve." When he clucked his tongue, his toothpick bobbled up and down. "The lettering becomes illegible, the wood decays and nothing remains to mark the spot for the loved ones."

"I ain't one."

"One what?" For an instant, Slocum thought he had the man's eyes caught, but they slipped away like they were greased.

"A loved one. How much for the stone?"

It came to ten dollars and Slocum paid the man. In the livery, he spent a few minutes getting reacquainted with the Appaloosa. The stall was filthy and the grain and water buckets were empty, so Slocum grained and watered the mare while he rubbed it down. Slocum took pains with his horses. More often than most men, he'd had to ride for his life and he didn't want to do that on a poor, neglected piece of horseflesh.

The sun was still hot, the air still good, and Slocum let the big mare pick its own way up the rutted, slippery street. It didn't like it too much—no horse likes

144

to put its feet where it can't be sure of the footing—but it didn't balk and wouldn't shy.

The Britannia corral was a large one, probably 30 feet on a side. Inside the corral, a kid was hunkered down beside one of the mine ponies, the tough little beasts that hauled the oar cars from the deep workings to the shaft. The pony was blind, of course; all the mine ponies went blind after a few years. The harnesses had galled this one. Slocum could see the deep red welts on its back. The kid was rubbing salve on the animal's sores, and Slocum watched for a minute.

The kid knew what he was doing. While he treated the pony's sensitive back, the animal had its head in a leather grain bucket, unworried. Slocum tied the Appaloosa to the top rail and eased himself over. He didn't get close to the kid, because no animal likes strangers nearby.

The corral was all mud and broken chunks of ice, chewed up by the horses' hooves. Horses are snobs: The Morgans stayed in one corner of the corral, holding themselves quite aloof from the mine ponies.

Slocum discounted most of the Morgans right away. One was very slightly lame, another's sides were heaving, like it had some sort of lung trouble, a couple were undersized and one needed shoeing. There wasn't anything very wrong with any of them. They'd all do in a pinch. But Slocum wanted the best.

He walked up slow, along the corral rail, so he wouldn't startle the Morgans or get them running about. When he got near enough, he relaxed against the rails and waited until, one by one, they gave up worrying about him and went back to their business. Slocum spotted two pregnant mares; one's belly had already dropped and it'd foal within the fortnight. Though Slocum could judge the individual animals pretty well, he wouldn't be able to guess how they'd work as a team. But, just watching, he could make some educated guesses. He figured that one big piebald was herd boss and another mare, a jet black, was its principal rival.

The kid planted himself right in front of Slocum and said, "Somethin' for you?"

"Name's Slocum. John Slocum. MacPherson told you I'd be coming by."

The kid nodded. "Yeah. He said you'd be needing four of these horses. Got any picked?"

"Thought you might help me out with that. Thought you might know 'em a sight better'n I do. I want the four best you got."

The kid pointed. "Well, the best leader we got is that big piebald over there. And next to her, the black."

The kid kept his eyes on the horses, studiously ignoring Slocum, but Slocum knew his answer wasn't quite so casual as it sounded. The kid wanted to find out if Slocum knew enough to be trusted with his horses.

"Yeah," Slocum said. "I expect if you hitched those two together, you'd have a real going concern."

The kid's face was blank and polite.

"Or a riot," Slocum continued.

And the kid stuck out his hand and Slocum shook it and they got down to business. Between them they picked a fine team, a team that'd pull together. Slocum asked him to have the team hitched up for the sled at MacPherson's house in the morning.

"Yeah," the kid said. "I'll be movin' all these horses out of here, anyway." He inspected the pale afternoon sky. "They should be getting here any time now."

"Who?"

"The whole damn town, that's who. This is where they hold the election."

The election had slipped Slocum's mind. He helped the kid move all the stock out of the main corral into the feeding corrals and helped him feed a good ration of hay and oats. The hay was clover, fine-stemmed, with plenty of dried clover flowers, and the oats were crisp and nutty without hulls or stones. He asked the kid to watch after his two packhorses. If he didn't come back by spring, the kid could keep them.

The citizens of Blue Rock began trickling up to the

Britannia corral. When the shift whistle blew at the mine, the trickle became a flood. The men lined up on the corral, and it reminded Slocum of a bull ring he'd seen in Mexico.

Most of the men were unusually quiet and sober. A few were puffing on pipes. They were doing their duty as citizens.

When Slocum finished feeding, he took his seat on the top rail with the rest. While he rolled himself a smoke, he passed the time guessing the nationalities of the miners in the crowd. He saw Welsh, Irish, Cornishmen, Italians, a few Scandinavians and two Chinese. A few men were dressed in their Sunday-go-to-meeting clothes, but most were in their coveralls. One candidate was already electioneering. He was a big man; he'd go 220 if he went an ounce, and he had the longest arms Slocum had ever seen. Another miner, a dark-haired, scar-faced gent, was on the other side of the corral doing a little campaigning of his own.

The election officials arrived in a bunch—Walker, MacPherson and MacPherson's mine foreman. The foreman was running the show.

"All right, you bunch of dumb muckers," the foreman shouted, "this is the election for sheriff, and whoever you pick you'll live with until this time next year, so quit your lallygaggin' and listen to me."

The miners hadn't been making much noise. Now they made less.

The foreman held up a sheaf of paper. "This here's the ballot. You write your choice on this ballot. I don't want no cheatin'. Any man who votes more than once, I'll give him his walkin' papers. Do you understand me?"

They did.

When Sheriff Hammer and George Ives arrived, they caused a little stir. They pushed a few miners off the corral to make room, and Hammer grinned his broadest grin and waved to the men who might be his friends. MacPherson's foreman glowered at him. "Sher-

147

iff, this ain't no time for electioneering and it won't do you no good. Them who'll vote for you will vote for you and the rest won't." He paused to scan the crowd.

Sheriff Hammer just kept on waving and smiling.

As the foreman passed out the ballots, he said, "And I don't want to see nobody voting for Abraham Lincoln or Robert E. Lee, either. Lincoln's dead and buried and Lee is not likely to ride to Blue Rock, Montana, to be your damn sheriff, so a vote for Lee is a vote wasted. Got me?" The miners were scribbling away. A few stared at their neighbors' ballots and poked fun. The men who couldn't write formed lines in front of MacPherson and Walker and whispered their choices, and the choices were recorded. The foreman prowled the corral, glowering suspiciously.

Slocum got a ballot, but he didn't put anything down on it. Hell, he didn't care who was sheriff of Blue Rock, Montana.

The foreman was gathering the ballots—snatching them from the slow writers and the slow deciders—when X. Beidler marched into the center of the corral. The man hunter's face was placid as ever, but Slocum knew he had something on his mind.

MacPherson and Walker counted the ballots. The foreman took the results and announced, "You have decided. Any man's name that I read has been officially nominated. When I read your name, stand in the corral. The last man still standing will be the new sheriff."

The list was short, just six names. Slocum didn't recognize the first two names, though he guessed that one fat man was on the list because he was shaking his head no, no, no, and his pals were trying to persuade him. The ape-armed miner was nominated and lightly sprang down. Likewise the wiry, scar-faced gent. It was no surprise to hear Sheriff Hammer's name or see his acceptance smile. He jumped down into the corral like a man who been in that muddy cockpit before.

148

"And receiving fifteen votes," the foreman read, "John Slocum."

Well, that was a hell of a note. One miner shouted, "Come on, Slocum, get down there." Another gave out a rebel yell. Slocum nodded his thanks and shook his head no thanks.

When everyone quieted down, the foreman repeated the rules. "No knives, clubs or guns. Dog eat dog. The last man still standing wins."

"Just a minute," Beidler said, and his quiet voice cut right through the mounting excitement. "Something you all ought to know. The road agents have struck again."

Well, that captured everyone's attention.

"A packer found Jim Thiel and his partner today. Robbed and killed. They had their throats cut. The bastards took the time to cut off Jim Thiel's balls."

A howl went up from the crowd. Jim Thiel had been a popular man. Beidler went on: "An Indian's been seen near the trail. A Blackfoot. Maybe he's in with the road agents. I don't know. Whoever they are"—he paused just long enough to put his eyes on Sheriff Hammer—"I'll get proof against them, and God help them then." He marched out of the corral.

The crowd hollered about Thiel for a moment, but they'd come here to watch an election and, by God, it couldn't start soon enough to suit them.

Sheriff Hammer stretched himself and threw a few mock punches at George Ives.

Slocum wasn't trying to think about Opal Hevener. He hardly ever thought about the dead. But when Beidler announced Jim Thiel's death, an image flashed before his mind: Opal Hevener's sad brown eyes. Slocum's hands were flexing themselves. He swallowed. He swallowed some of his rage because it threatened to swallow him. He told his body to wait a bit, to save it up. His brain got icy cold and everything he saw snapped into sharper detail, like the world had been repainted by a more skilled artist with a better technique and more expressive brush. He saw the clean lines of the corral rails and the smudge where a miner's boot had marred the paint. He saw the tiny scrap of horse manure on his boot. He looked at the rich blandness of Sheriff Hammer's smile. All the teeth in the world and above them the eyes of a pig. Though he didn't know it, Slocum was smiling, too. The miners who saw his smile looked away real fast and found something to talk to their neighbors about.

When Slocum dropped into the corral, he landed lightly, his hands loose and easy at his side. He moved so quickly and quietly that nobody noticed the new candidate for a full ten seconds. A few miners cheered, but Slocum didn't hear them. The odds on Sheriff Hammer dropped from three to one to even money. Slocum didn't hear the betting, either.

Pharoah MacPherson saw Slocum's move and thought about Lucia and was worried for her.

Walker had been wondering how many barrels of whiskey to break out after the election. When Slocum jumped down, he upped the estimate by one full barrel. It would be little enough to slake a citizen's thirst on a grand day like today.

Slocum tucked his pants into his boot tops. The sun was fading and there was a definite winter chill in the air. A couple of crows flew overhead, singing their raucous song. The air bit at Slocum's lungs. It was so thin, at this altitude, he never seemed to get enough of it. He looked at Hammer's barrel chest. Hammer'd be able to get more good out of the air than Slocum could.

The scar-faced gent was running in place, just like a pugilist. The long-armed miner bent over and touched the ground a few times. With those arms, he could stand a mile away and batter you to death.

When George Ives tapped the sheriff on the shoulder, he turned around, puzzled. When he saw Slocum in the arena, at first he frowned and then he smiled his best smile and gave Slocum a big wink.

Good. He's overconfident.

The scar-faced gent was throwing punches—fast, very fast, but not much steam in them.

Soon all four of them were facing one another in a loose square. Everyone's eyes ranged over the other three. In a fight like this, a man could be an ally one minute and in the next, he'd be trying to rip your arm off.

"All right," the foreman yelled. "Let's go. May the best man win."

The very next moment, all hell broke loose.

Sheriff Hammer went for Scarface with a tremendous bellow. Ape Arms charged Slocum. Slocum back-pedaled swiftly, catching Ape Arms' blows on his forearms and shoulders. Slocum heard those long arms go whistling past his ear and the grunts the man made: *uh, uh, uh.*

Sheriff Hammer tried to slam Scarface into the ground, where the sheriff's greater weight would have some advantage, but Scarface slipped around him and drove a couple of quick shots into the sheriff's kidneys. With the sheriff temporarily out of the way, he took his chance at Slocum's opponent's unprotected back. Scarface put one pointy-toed boot into Ape Arms' back, just at the base of the spine, and wheeled to face the sheriff again. The sheriff had recovered faster than Scarface'd figured, and the smaller man only had time to bounce a couple of blows off Hammer's hard midriff before Hammer ran him down like an ore train. The two men went down in the mud, Scarface still punching and the sheriff grappling for his throat.

Slocum saw the kick delivered and watched Ape Arms' face go gray. The next looping punch was wide, so Slocum stepped inside and fired three quick shots at the man's diaphragm. He almost got back outside again, but Ape Arm caught him with a left that took skin off his cheek and made his face go numb. When Ape Arms pressed his advantage, Slocum slipped inside again with a volley of lefts and rights and was back outside again before Ape Arms could recover.

Sheriff Hammer was covered with mud, and Scarface was, too. Scarface scuttled desperately away from the bigger man, but each time he'd almost get to his feet, the sheriff would grab an ankle and pull him down again. Scarface kicked Hammer in the face, and though it wasn't a hard kick, it blurred the sheriff's vision and Scarface was up in an instant and dancing away. The sheriff got to one knee and waited. Scarface danced around him, and the sheriff kept pivoting, one knuckle on the ground, like a runner waiting for the starting gun. When Hammer finally lunged, he was a bit dizzy and about a foot wide of the mark. Scarface laughed as the sheriff roared by and hit him twice on the back of the neck.

Slocum was having trouble with Ape Arms. The taller man had backed Slocum into a corner and was tagging him pretty frequently. They weren't killer punches, but they weren't feather pillows, either. Slocum was staying real busy.

When the sheriff got up, he shook his head like he was checking to see if everything was still working up there. Scarface figured he'd hurt him real bad. When the sheriff charged again, Scarface stood his ground, his fists flashing at the sheriff's gut. Once more the sheriff rolled right over him and this time he got hold of an arm to bend.

Scarface was shrieking, but his other arm was still working, punching at Sheriff Hammer's belly, trying for his balls. Hammer twisted his leg to cover his genitals while he worked the man's arm. Scarface's shrieking rose an octave or two, and the watchers heard a dull snap.

The sheriff got up slowly and brushed some of the mud off his face. He inspected his knuckles. Scarface was kneeling in the mud. When he got to his feet, he was gray-faced and his right arm hung uselessly at his side.

Some miner yelled, "Twenty on the sheriff," and one of Scarface's backers yelled that he should fuck himself.

Sheriff Hammer smiled at Scarface in a kindly, fatherly way. "You're still on your feet," he reminded him. Then Hammer stepped in real close and landed three or four punches on the injured man's rib cage. Scarface had his good hand up, but he couldn't do much with just one mitt. Sheriff Hammer back-pedaled and caught his breath. "The last man on his feet is the winner," he said, and tried a kick for the other man's balls, but Scarface took it on the thigh. Still game, he whipped a left into Hammer's face and cut him. Hammer put a hand to his face, saw the blood, smiled his smile and kicked Scarface's broken arm.

Scarface went down to one knee and the sheriff walked a couple steps off. He looked at the man kneeling in the mud. "Well," he observed, "you ain't on your feet now. That's something." He wiped his hand across his face again and came away with a little more blood.

George Ives yelled from the sidelines, "He ain't out yet, Sheriff! He ain't done."

The sheriff said calmly, "Course he ain't done," and took three long steps forward and kicked Scarface under the chin like he was kicking a field goal. The man came up off the ground, arced backward and landed flat in the mud. His head was way back at a funny angle, and when he landed, the crowd could hear him voiding himself.

"Now he's done," the sheriff noted.

Slocum felt like a man inside a blizzard. He was a little faster than Ape Arms and his punches packed more sting, but the long-armed bastard kept serving them up, one after another, and it was all Slocum could do to stay clear and get in a few licks of his own. He didn't mind drawing it out. He figured to step in pretty soon and work the man's midsection. A couple of doses of that should wrap it up. Trouble was, he was losing his wind.

Slocum barely saw the sheriff coming. He was running with the astonishing speed very big men sometimes have. The sheriff piled onto Ape Arms' back and rode him forward, and Slocum just got out of the way before the two men crashed into the corral. A few miners fell off and landed in a heap. In one ferocious motion, the sheriff grabbed Ape Arms by the hair and smashed his face against the bottom rail, breaking his nose; smashing his face again, he broke his cheekbone. When Ape Arms went limp, the sheriff rolled off and faced Slocum.

He smiled that big smile and this time his pig eyes were smiling, too. "Looks like it's me and you, boy," he said. "I done finished off all the real fighters."

For some reason, Slocum reached out and slapped Hammer across the face. He could have made it a good punch, but he slapped him instead.

The sheriff bellowed and jumped over Ape Arms' body, and Slocum let him come. The sheriff had both arms outstretched. Slocum grabbed his wrists and sat down. He put his boot in the sheriff's belly. The sheriff was coming very fast and he flew. Slocum held onto his wrists as the bigger man went on over his head, and when he figured the bird had flown far enough and gathered enough momentum, Slocum jerked straight down. The sheriff's head smashed into the ground as his heels continued blissfully on their way. Slocum was up before the sheriff recovered his wits. Slocum got off a couple of kicks. Good ones.

When Sheriff Hammer got to his feet, he was crippled and slowed. John Slocum was whipping punches into his face and the blood was running into his eyes and he couldn't see so good. He roared like a bull until one of Slocum's punches caught him in the throat and then he wasn't roaring, he was gagging.

Slocum looked at the wreck he was facing. Still brute strong, still dangerous, but hurt. Hurt bad.

Slocum thought that Opal Hevener was a real sweet girl.

And he chopped Sheriff Hammer into the mud like a man chops a tree.

9

The great gold nugget tottered on the prybars. Slocum was straining against the steel bar and the bar was bending, and if the nugget slipped, it'd crush somebody sure as hell. Slocum grunted and found a few more ounces of strength to throw against the bar, and the heavy nugget finally tilted and rolled forward with a crash onto the tarp they'd spread over MacPherson's floor. Even with the house's reinforced flooring, the building shook and a few streams of dust trickled out of the wainscoting.

As Slocum set the point of his bar under the nugget again, MacPherson said, "Why didn't you take the sheriff's job?"

Slocum nodded to the miners who'd been prying with him and they heaved, three sets of sinews working as one, and the nugget rolled again. This time they were closer to the outside sill and the house didn't shake so bad.

Slocum wiped the dust off his face, smiled at the mine manager and said, "Me—a sheriff? Why turn a silk purse into a sow's ear?" He and the miners rolled the nugget again.

When they had it outside, on the ramp to the sled, Slocum double-checked everything. If the damn thing came off the ramp, it'd take a block and tackle to get it back again. MacPherson nattered on: "Now Blue Rock'll have to hold another election. And chances are altogether too good that Hammer will win it."

"You want him, you can have him," Slocum snapped. "Once we get this gold to Fort Bozeman, I'm travelin' on. I got no business here."

Three miners had been detailed to help Slocum. At first they'd regarded the huge nugget with awe, running their callused hands over its smooth golden surface like a man caresses a woman. Once they started moving it, it became more ordinary: just a big damn rock—no more.

MacPherson said, "I hope you boys know you're making history this morning. Think of it: the Biggest Gold Nugget in the World."

One of the miners spat in his hand, set his bar and said, "I wonder if we rolled the damn thing into Walkers' how many drinks it would buy."

MacPherson scoffed. "Hell, man, with this you could buy the entire saloon, kit and kaboodle."

The nugget tottered on the ramp, and Slocum had to pry on the down side to hold it. Finally, with a crash that startled the horses, the 2,000-pound stone settled onto the sled.

The miner grinned at MacPherson and said, "Walker can keep the joint. I ain't no damn saloon keeper."

In her traveling outfit, Lucia MacPherson looked like an English countrywoman dressed for an outing. The snow was already starting to dust her neat green pillbox hat. As the miners left, they nodded respectfully to her and one touched his cap. The four big Morgans were steaming in the snow and the leader was pawing with his forefoot.

Slocum tightened the chains around the rock, checking and rechecking them. If the nugget shifted and fell off the sled, they'd never get it back on again.

With the practiced hands of an old campaigner, MacPherson lashed his personal gear to the sled. Slocum rolled himself a smoke. The snow was falling heavy, and the clouds looked like they held a lot more where that came from. Slocum sniffed at the air, smelled the curious, almost electrical charge in it. "Blizzard coming," he remarked laconically. "A bad one."

MacPherson squinted up at the sky. "We can leave tomorrow," he said. "If this gets worse, we won't be able to see where we're going."

The visibility had closed down to 100 feet. If the wind picked up, the driver wouldn't be able to see his lead horses. But Slocum knew the road agents would be after this cargo for sure. And in this weather they wouldn't be able to see any better than he could. Besides, if things got real bad, they could dig a snow cave and wait it out. Since a snow cave is wet, cold and constricting, Slocum didn't mention it. But it was an alternative if things went real sour. "You got everything?" Slocum asked. "If we're gonna get, let's get."

The manager dashed back into the house as fast as his wooden leg allowed him.

Lucia perched herself on the sled. "Will it get worse?"

"Likely."

She nodded brusquely and changed the subject. "Yesterday at the fight, Mr. Beidler was a study in confusion. At the last, when only you and the sheriff were fighting, he made a bet. He bet on you."

"Yeah. Well, a man doesn't always back his sentimental favorite."

MacPherson returned with the cased London Colts and slipped them under the seat with a flourish. "Primed and ready, Slocum," he announced.

Slocum led the Morgans down to the Britannia's blasting shed. He chose a case of dynamite: the 60 per cent. He hefted the sticks to see if the nitro had started to seep out of the bottom.

The powderman watched him curiously. "You handled the stuff before, eh?"

"Some," Slocum admitted. He handled the blasting caps with real reverence. They were fulminate of mercury—the same stuff they used to prime pistol cartridges—and they were touchy as hell. He set the dynamite on the front of the sled, and after wrapping the caps with a couple of old soft shirts, he set them on the very back. If the caps blew, they'd set the dynamite off anyway, but the separation made Slocum feel some better, as if he'd done everything he could.

MacPherson took the reins. The sled bumped along the rutty road, and Slocum was glad he'd padded the caps.

A few miners peered through the windows of Walker's Saloon as the party rode by. Through the swirling snow, they could just make out the sled and Slocum out front on his Appaloosa. Slocum had a ten-gauge Greener tucked under his arm like he wanted to use it. A few wiser heads backed away from Walker's window. Slocum had a reputation and so did the Greener: "One barrel cuts a man in half and the other makes a crowd out of him."

X. Beidler saw them leave. He thought he'd give them a few hours' start before he followed.

Once they were outside of town on a clear trail, Slocum breathed a little easier. Shotgun or no shotgun, narrow streets made him uncomfortable. Too many windows. He swapped the Greener for his Colt rifle. He wanted the Colt's greater range.

The wind was gusting the falling snow. It slapped them in the face and found its way past all the mufflers, the tightly buttoned collars, onto their cold necks.

Soon enough the trail was winding its way through densely packed pines on the side of the mountain. Though great snowfields lay above them, Slocum wasn't worried about avalanches. He was worried that the Morgans might twist an ankle in the deepening snow, and got down to help them over the rough spots.

The avalanches wouldn't come today. It was too cold. Slocum kept his mind on the horses. He didn't say anything when he spotted the tracks of two horses in a protected hummock beside the trail. No sense worrying everyone.

The sled was moving through an endless white tunnel. They had only 20 yards of visibility on both sides. From habit, Slocum rested the Colt on his hip and his eyes kept moving from side to side, seeking the first flash of movement, listening for man sound.

Lucia MacPherson began to sing, "Dashing through the snow, on a one-horse open sleigh . . ."

Slocum snapped, "Shut the hell up," and Lucia was hurt, because she had been trying to cheer up a singularly cheerless journey.

The tracks meant someone would be waiting. And Slocum had given his word.

158

John Slocum had had most things taken from him. The war took his youth. The carpetbaggers got his homeplace. The law took his chance to go through the world as an ordinary man: loving a woman, raising a family. All he owned was his freedom—his ability to say absolutely yes or absolutely no. A man's word is what he is. And John Slocum, though he never would have boasted on it, would rather have died than go back on his word.

And so Slocum rode through the driving snow and rubbed the snow off his eyebrows and squinted against the storm, with his Colt resting on his hip and his cold finger on a trigger he'd promised not to pull.

They pulled up the horses at midday. Slocum had wanted to make a little more distance before they stopped, but here the trail was blocked by shattered tree trunks and the debris of a recent avalanche. A single horse could clamber over the slide, but the sled and the team were too wide to make it.

Slocum got out the feed bags while Lucia unwrapped the sandwiches she'd packed that morning. Slocum wolfed his down, his eyes constantly scanning the terrain. This was too fine an ambush spot. He warned MacPherson to keep a sharp lookout while he cleared a path for the sled.

By the time the sun was an hour further in the sky, Slocum had cut out a new trail big enough for the team. It was tricky getting the horses through the jumble, but with MacPherson at the reins and Slocum working the lead Morgan, they made it across without incident. Ahead, the trail widened below the brow of a sparsely forested ridge.

MacPherson turned to Lucia to say, "That was a bit too near for—"

Whatever else he said was lost in the sound of a high, bone-chilling scream. It froze the manager stiff in his seat. Rigid, he saw Slocum dive behind the horses. The scream was still echoing among the hills when Lucia heard a funny little *whap* sound and, half a second later, the boom of a heavy rifle.

MacPherson shoved her off the sled, with a curious, half-lunging motion, and covered her. He lay across her, sprawled heavily.

When Slocum heard the scream, he ducked under the horses, that fast. He'd heard that scream before. Heard it at Adobe Wells and outside Fort Kearny. It was the last sound Custer heard at the Little Big Horn: the war cry of the Plains Indian. The scream gave Slocum time to duck before the air over his head was filled with flying lead.

His eyes were aimed upslope and his finger was tense on the trigger, but what the hell good would it do him?

Two guns working on the ridge. One—a Winchester, by the sound of it—was raking the sled, throwing chips, gouging the great block of gold. The other had the big hollow boom of a Sharps. Most of the fire was going high, since the ambushers were firing downhill. The stand of pines that concealed the gunman was scrub jack pine, nowhere near dense enough to hide a man. Behind the puffs of powder smoke, Slocum saw a couple of shapes: Hammer and Ives, he figured.

Why the hell didn't I kill those two when I had a chance? I should have wrung their necks like a couple chickens.

Slocum was sprawled along the bank, only 200 yards below the guns. Now and again a near shot would throw a gout of snow over him, but that was just annoying.

He hefted the Colt. They were just at the edge of his range. Too bad. With the Winchester, he could have combed their hair. "Well, hell," Slocum muttered, "I only promised not to shoot nobody. I never said I wouldn't jostle them a bit."

He picked his spots: one on each side of the Winchester; three right over the Sharps rifleman's head. The Colt roared five times, as fast as he could shoot it. Slocum reloaded. The fire above him had slackened off. *I guess the bullets went where I wanted,* Slocum thought. *Maybe I been underrating this Colt.*

Once more he picked his spots and once more the

Colt roared. The Sharps stopped. The Winchester stopped. Somebody yelled. Slocum thumbed the bright cartridges in. Somebody yelled, "Goddammit! Let's haul our asses out of here!"

Slocum laid on another barrage, aiming to come just as close as he dared. He guessed it was close enough, because he heard their horses start up and glimpsed them flashing through the trees toward the ridge top.

Slocum reloaded. It got very quiet. The wind whispered. One of the Morgans was stamping nervously. Lucia was sobbing. Slocum sat for a few minutes. He was pretty sure the road agents wouldn't return, but Boot Hill was full of men who'd been pretty sure. Finally, he brushed the snow off his pants and walked back to the sled. The MacPhersons hadn't returned fire and he knew what he'd find.

Lucia had her uncle's head in her lap and was rocking him as she might have rocked her own baby.

Slocum said, "Oh, hell."

The hole in Pharoah MacPherson's breastbone was about the size of a man's thumb. The exit hole would be the size of a dinner plate. Sharps .69—nothing else made a hole like that. Slocum said "Oh, hell" again and knelt beside the girl.

She was in a daze. Her tear-streaked face was staring at the snow and her hand was mechanically patting the dead man's hair into place. Gently Slocum lifted the dead man and laid him on the sled. He helped Lucia to her feet.

The bullets hadn't done much damage to the sled, though there were some bright new splashes in the gold and a chip in a ringbolt next to the blasting caps. *Another inch to the left. . . ,* Slocum thought, and shrugged it away. Life was full of near things.

Lucia was standing beside the sled, not really seeing anything. Slocum said, "He was a good man, but now he's gone and there ain't no way you can bring him back again." She didn't seem to hear him.

He lashed the body to the ringbolts, wondering, as

always, how the smallest men got heavy as lead once the life went out of them.

Though it was only four o'clock, the snow was falling pretty heavily and it'd be dark in an hour. Slocum cracked the heavy stockman's whip and shouted "Gee-up," and the Morgans strained against the harness to break the frozen sled runners free. Lucia sat beside Slocum like a bundle of grief, and from time to time he felt her shoulders tremble.

When the trail flattened and widened, at the mouth of a small brush-choked valley, he hauled savagely at the reins and urged the Morgans into the deeper snow off the trail. They smashed through to their fetlocks.

When the valley opened up, the going got easier, though the snow was still very deep and the powerful horses' muscles were heaving with strain. Slocum found a lonely clump of Douglas firs that rose out of the snow like an island.

He got down and lashed poles for an Indian burial couch, suspended between four tall trees like a wooden hammock. Without thinking about it, he built it the Indian way, with Indian lashings, and faced it toward the west, where the sun's dying rays could show the dead warrior the land of his ancestors. He collected MacPherson's body and arranged him on the couch, his buffalo coat buttoned to the throat and his eyes wide open for the dangerous journey he would make. He put one of MacPherson's London Colts in the dead man's hand so he would not be defenseless as he made his way through the spirit land.

Lucia watched Slocum's preparations apathetically until he took her hand and asked, "You got any prayers for him?" And she shook her head no and wept. Wept with her sorrow coming out of her in dark, cleansing waves. When her sobbing quieted some, Slocum cast a last glance at the figure on the couch and touched the brim of his hat in farewell.

Later on, Slocum found another valley that led still deeper into the mountains. Lucia sat huddled on the seat while he smashed through the deep snow, hauling on the leader's traces.

All of a sudden Lucia became aware that they were stopped. Slocum was talking to a man—an Indian, by the look of him—who'd simply materialized out of the dark and falling snow. Then they were moving again, but now two men were hauling on the traces, bullying the horses forward. Gray men, half obscured in the driving snow. The sled stopped before a small cabin. A welcoming glow shone through its oiled butcher-paper windows.

"Come on," Slocum said. "If you sit there all night, you'll freeze to death sure." She did try to get up. She did try. But her legs were too numb and she'd sobbed away too much of her strength. Slocum carried her inside as if she were a child.

Voices were murmuring in some high musical dialect Lucia felt she should understand but just couldn't. When her eyes cleared, she saw two Indian women and an Indian child watching her with bright curiosity in their eyes. The older of the two women was offering her a bowl of soup—clear soup with chunks of something floating in it. She didn't want to eat, wasn't hungry, didn't want any of the disgusting stuff, but drank it down, every bit, picking the meat out with her fingers. The older woman smiled a toothless, blackened smile and offered her more. She drank that, too.

The cabin's walls were draped with Indian blankets and hides from a wickiup. The hides broke the wind; inside, the air was dead still. Pine knots in the fireplace were hissing and popping. Slocum was signing to the Indian brave, and the brave kept repeating the same sign back: a sweeping motion from his chest outward. The chattering women were stuffing their buckskin parfleches, and, with a grunt, the older shouldered her load and went out. The other Indians followed, man, woman and child.

"Where are they going?" Lucia asked.

163

Slocum shrugged. "They've given us their home for the night."

Lucia wrinkled her brow. "We could all have stayed. They didn't need to go out into the storm."

"He'll have someplace in mind where they can hole up. A cave maybe."

"That's crazy. John, you go after them and bring them back here!"

Slocum stirred the fire. "He'd be real insulted," he replied quietly. "One time when I was staying with the Blackfeet, up near Going-to-the-Sun, a man from another camp felt he owed me something. His camp was a couple days' ride from ours. When he showed up, it was a nice spring morning. We talked. We smoked. He gave me his best horse."

Lucia was puzzled. "So?"

"Then he walked all the way home. Blackfeet believe a gift is only worth what it costs the giver."

Slocum was stuffing tobacco into a long Indian pipe. The stem was hard-fired yellow clay and the bowl was green soapstone, blackened from years of use. Slocum lit it with a coal and, as if it was his usual habit, offered the pipe to the four directions before he took his smoke. He smiled at her. "It's kinnikinnick," he said. "Indian tobacco. You've seen those low, sharp-leaved plants in the spring? The ones with the tiny red berries?"

Soon the room was filled with a sweet pungency that seemed to seep from the trappings on the walls. It made Lucia very drowsy, and almost, not quite, she started to dream. Almost, but not quite, she dreamed of other campsites, other times, with dusky-skinned children laughing and plenty of game hanging from the tripods behind the camp.

She freed her long hair, and with the firelight dancing on her lovely fine features, she unbuttoned her coat, tossed her blouse into the corner and stood before John Slocum, naked to the waist. Her breasts were golden in the light. Her nipples were so hard they hurt her. "John," she said quietly, "come here. I want you."

"Now, there's a good idea," Sheriff Hammer said.

George Ives just giggled.

When Slocum came boiling to his feet, the big sheriff simply cocked the hammers of the shotgun he held against Lucia MacPherson's naked back, and Slocum stopped in his tracks, petrified.

The two men had slipped inside the cabin behind the heavy robes, and if Slocum moved, the first barrel would kill Lucia and the second would finish him in a wink.

"Sit down, Slocum." The sheriff gestured expansively with his left hand, but the hand holding the shotgun didn't budge an inch.

Slocum sat down.

"That's better. A whole lot better. I hate to see a man gettin' himself all uncomfortable when he don't have to." The sheriff was marked some by Slocum's beating, but he was moving well enough.

Lucia tried to cover her breasts.

George Ives giggled. "Look at her, sheriff. Look at them titties."

The sheriff smiled. "They *are* handsome. Ma'am, you have my compliments."

"Our Indian friends just stepped out to get firewood," Lucia lied. "When they return, the braves will tear you apart. If you leave immediately, we won't tell them you were here."

"Was that sorry little fucker a brave?" the sheriff asked. He kept his eyes glued on Slocum, and the muzzle never wavered from Lucia's back. George had his pistol drawn and was sighting at Slocum's head like a man at target range.

Slocum's mind was churning, working, looking for *any* way out. He was having no luck. No matter what he did, Lucia would surely die.

Maybe the sheriff was reading Slocum's thought, because he wiggled his big thumb on the shotgun hammer and said, "I'd hate to see you make a move, Slocum. I'd hate to see you wiggle. You just roll over now and put your hands behind your back where Georgie can hog-tie you."

It was a defeat as bitter as any John Slocum had ever suffered. He wanted to fling himself at them, but Lucia . . . Lucia. He put his face against the dirt floor, and George wrapped his hands with pigging strings. He wrapped them real tight, and the rawhide cut Slocum's circulation. Slocum rolled back upright, his back to the wall. As soon as his hands were out of sight, he was trying to force the lashings apart. All his great muscles were working, but his face was disinterested and nothing showed of a struggle that threatened to burst his heart.

"That Indian buck weren't no brave," the sheriff asserted. "Hell, he cried like a baby when Georgie cut the kid's throat."

George was anxious to set the record straight. "Yeah, but the little fucker was brave enough when his turn came. He spit in your face, sheriff. He spit right in your face."

The sheriff rubbed his face with the back of his hand and growled, "If you'd kept hold of him like I told you, he never would have. You was holdin' his neck and the damn knife. How the hell did you let him get away from you?"

George laughed. "He didn't get too far."

"If I thought you let him loose on purpose, I'd use this shotgun on you, Georgie, partner or no partner."

George stopped laughing. He muttered, "I reckon you'll use it on me anyway—someday when I ain't no help to you no more."

Immediately the sheriff was contrite. "Oh, hell, Georgie, don't go on like that. I'd never do you that way. We're buddies, ain't we?" And he laughed.

Slocum thought George had it right. Someday the sheriff *would* use that shotgun on him. He'd probably feel bad about it afterward, too.

"Well," George said, "if you hadn't got so mad, we could have had that Indian woman. The old bag wasn't no use, but you didn't have to lose your temper like that. It was just a little spit, for Christ's sake. And you

166

know you kept on stabbin' those women once they was dead. You was like a crazy man."

"What'd you call me?" the sheriff's voice was small—small as a little rattlesnake in that quiet room. George's face went white and he put up one hand like he could catch the deadly charge of buckshot and said, "I didn't mean nothin' by it. You know I didn't mean nothin'. I was just disappointed. I ain't had no pussy since we flattened Opal. Indian pussy ain't bad, either. I heard some men say they wouldn't have no Indian pussy if it came on a silver platter, but I never minded it myself. But," he added judiciously, "sometimes they smell kind of bad. It's that bear grease they put on their skin. I always wash my privates after."

John Slocum was focused. His entire body, his whole strength was focused on the rawhide strips that bound his hands. He just needed enough room to slip his hands through. The thin strands were cutting deep into his flesh, but they weren't giving—not one inch.

Lucia casually walked over and picked up her blouse. One of the London Colts was inside the buckskin pouch by the wall. She could picture it in her mind. She knew how it'd feel in her hand.

"No need puttin' that shirt on, miss." The sheriff's voice stopped her. "You'll just be takin' it off again."

Lucia's heart skipped a beat, but she didn't panic. Deliberately, she dropped her blouse beside the buckskin pouch. If their attention was distracted for just a second . . .

George put his pistol back in his belt. He lit a smoke.

"Nice gun," Slocum observed.

George grinned, hauled the gun out again and pretended to inspect it. "Yeah, ain't it a honey? You don't see too many of these London Colts." He stuck it back in his belt.

The sheriff smiled. "We found MacPherson. Sure we did. I'm a little surprised at you, Slocum, buryin' a white man that way."

George patted his breast pocket. "I got his watch.

167

Hell, a dead man can't tell time." He spat in the fire.

Slocum desperately wanted to keep them talking. He wanted a little time. "Beidler'll be on your trail," he said. "They say he never gives up. He followed Kid Curry into the hole in the wall country and hung the kid under the noses of his friends." Slocum's hands were bleeding. The blood was seeping under his buttocks.

The sheriff unloaded his shotgun and leaned it against the wall where Lucia couldn't get it. As he spoke, he was peeling off his heavy buffalo coat. "He won't be lookin' for us, John. He'll be lookin' for you. You shouldn't have murdered MacPherson with that Sharps rifle of yours. Hell, the Sharps leaves a hole a blind man would recognize." He tossed his coat in the corner and began working the buttons on his flannel shirt. "And any damn fool knows he can't go committin' murders and leavin' notes around. Now"—he waggled his finger like a schoolmaster—"I know. I done murdered twenty men—or was it thirty?"

George thought. His lips moved and his fingers did, too. Finally he said, "Closer to thirty, I'd say. And that don't count Indians or that nigger stableman."

The sheriff was disgusted. "You can't count niggers and Indians, George."

George was defiant. "I *know* that," he snapped. "I said it was closer to thirty *not* countin' Indians and niggers." He found a pint of whiskey, unscrewed the cap, shuddered and offered the bottle to Lucia. "Here you are, ma'am. You better drink some of this. I reckon you'll need it."

Lucia waved him away. "What note?" she asked.

The sheriff tossed his shirt on top of the coat and scratched at his filthy yellow long underwear. "Ahhhh," he said. "The note Slocum left pinned to your uncle's chest," he explained. "The one that said: 'X. Beidler, thanks for the gold, John Slocum.'" He waited for Lucia to admire his cleverness. When she didn't, he shrugged, said "No matter" and unbuckled his belt.

George was excited. "Even without the note, that gold'll take us way out of Beidler's reach. Two thousand pounds of gold will buy a lot of distance. Hell, we would have taken it when we ambushed you but for that damn Indian yelling like that. Gave me the creeps he did. I'm glad he can't yell no more." George pushed the whiskey bottle at Lucia. She didn't want any; couldn't he see that? She pushed his hand away.

George's sudden slap almost knocked her down. Roughly he pushed the bottle at her. Slocum's face was bone white and the blood was welling from his wrists and he was praying the wet rawhide would slip just a little.

Heavily the sheriff sat down and tugged at his high boots with a grunt for each boot. He wore a red sock on one foot and a dirty gray one on the other. When he saw her staring at them, with a curiously boyish smile he explained, "Folks never see your feet unless you have your boots off. And by the time you got 'em off, it don't matter very much."

The sight of the mismatched socks cleared Lucia's brain. The little touch of foolishness in the big, dangerous sheriff reduced him to more human proportions. *He's just a man,* she thought. *He killed Uncle Pharoah and he'll kill John and you, too, unless you can kill him first. Lucia, be clever!*

She smiled a most fetching smile at George and said, "Excuse me. I was forgetting my manners." She took the bottle from the bewildered George Ives and took a sip of the searing whiskey. It jolted her and started her mind working double time. With a steady hand, she started unfastening her skirt.

Slocum would have felt better dead.

The sheriff was down to his long johns and he stepped out of them, too, saying *"There!"* Like he was revealing a great work of art. His heavy, pimply gut. His cock, already swelling in self-admiration.

Lucia forced herself to say huskily, "You're quite a man, sheriff. *Quite* a man."

169

He swelled with the compliment.

Oh, Jesus, she thought.

"Damn it, sheriff," George whined. "Why do you always get to go first? You went first with Opal and now with this one."

"Because I'm the boss," the sheriff explained.

Lucia wanted to be over by the buckskin pouch. Oh, how she wanted it. She licked her lips. "I can be very good for you, Sheriff Hammer. I can be *very* good." She glanced at a pile of sleeping robes by the wall. "Do you mind if I put some of those down?" She made herself laugh, and though it rang awfully close to hysteria to her ears, the sheriff didn't detect any false note. "I'd like to have a little something under me, with a big man like you on top."

"Sure thing." He gestured expansively. "Make yourself comfortable." As she spread the blankets right next to the buckskin pouch, he was fondling himself. She folded the blankets. God, if her heart kept pounding this way, it would surely burst.

Slocum could twist his wrists now, back and forth, back and forth. He was working the rawhide, soaking it in his blood. Did it give a little? Just the slightest bit?

Lucia MacPherson stepped out of her underthings and faced the sheriff with a welcoming smile on her lips and a fierce prayer in her heart. *Let me kill him, God. Let me be thy instrument.*

She was beautiful standing there, and George Ives gaped openly.

Absently the sheriff stroked his cock.

"I'm not getting any younger," she said.

"Sure," he said. "Sure."

She lay on the pile of blankets and he got on top of her; it felt like a hog was on top of her, but she kissed him anyway. He didn't seem very interested in kissing. He pushed his finger into her.

"Oh," she said. "Oh, oh." But she was dead cold inside. George's face was getting a slight glaze on it, and pretty soon she could let her hand sort of casually flop over on the buckskin pouch and . . .

The sheriff grunted when he entered her. It hurt but not too bad and she moaned and he was bucking his hips into her. *Christ! What a heavy bastard!*

Slocum watched the sheriff's flabby ass heaving and felt the rawhide give a little. Slocum hadn't prayed since he was eight years old, but he was praying now for that rawhide to break. The sheriff was fumbling with Lucia's breasts like he couldn't get enough of her. Lucia's hands were flopping from side to side. She was moaning and her hands kept tempo with the moans. Slocum saw her left hand slip inside the buckskin pouch. He felt a sudden surge of hope and the rawhide gave a little more.

The sheriff was thinking they'd keep this one alive for a few days. He hadn't had anything this good in years. He stopped thinking when he felt the circle of cold steel against his head.

"Stop," Lucia said calmly.

He stopped. "Oh," he said. For the very first time, he looked into Lucia MacPherson's cold blue eyes and he said "Oh" again. He lay quite still. He shriveled.

George stood stock-still for an instant before his hand started creeping toward his gun.

"Mr. Ives," Lucia said, "this is a Colt revolver and I am a crack shot. Now, I want you to drop your pistol on the floor. I am no gunman. Therefore, if you do anything the slightest bit out of the ordinary, I'm afraid I shall misinterpret your intentions and put a bullet in your brain."

In slow motion, George Ives extracted the Colt with his forefinger and thumb and slowly, ever so slowly, bent over and set it on the floor. Soon enough he and the sheriff would turn the tables and he didn't want to ruin a good pistol by dropping it. Good firearms were hard to come by.

"Put your hands at your sides," Lucia instructed the sheriff. "Unfortunately, this pistol has a very light trigger, and if you jostle me in any way, I'm afraid there'll be an accident."

171

The sheriff moved his hands to his sides. He lay on Lucia MacPherson like a side of beef.

"You may roll off now," she said, quite pleasantly.

The sheriff obeyed. It made him want to laugh. She was a saucy wench. She'd be lots of fun once they got that gun away from her.

"Just keep rolling, sheriff. That's right. Right up against that wall."

George knew Lucia couldn't watch both of them at once. Her eyes were flickering back and forth as, unsteadily, she got to her haunches. George was real eager.

Lucia's bullet took him in the right eye.

The shot was very loud. The bullet passed right through George's skull and he dropped to his knees like a supplicant before he toppled forward. He voided himself very noisily. The cabin stank.

Slocum had worked one of his hands almost free. He kept his eyes on Lucia's calm face and kept twisting the rawhide.

Sheriff Hammer was trying to press himself through the wall. He was sliding up the wall to his feet. His hands were in front of his chest.

For some reason, Lucia said "Excuse me," before she shot him in the balls.

His scream crashed against Slocum's ears. He started flipping around the cabin floor, clutching at his groin, and the blood spouted out of him like water out of a burst hose. He was thrashing, doubling up, shrieking and kicking. Lucia stepped over his thrashing legs, collected George's pistol, stepped over him again, went to the water bucket and started cleaning herself.

"Oh, please," Hammer said, "please help . . ."

Lucia had all her attention on her cleaning. The sheriff was flopping around again like a dying fish. The blood was all over the cabin, and when Lucia went to get her clothes, she had to step cautiously.

Slocum's hands were finally free. He was stiff when he got up and his hands hurt. When he put his hands in the water bucket, they ran red. The cuts were very

172

deep. He flexed them, and though they hurt, they'd be good as new someday.

The sheriff's eyes were rolled back in his head and his hands were pressed to his ruined testicles like he could do something about it. He had white foam on his mouth.

Lucia stood in the center of the cabin, clothes in hand, staring at nothing. Slocum touched the gun she still held in her hand. "Finish it," he said. "Enough."

The gun lifted in her hand and it was like she didn't even notice it and she never remembered pulling the trigger, but there was a loud report and the sheriff bounced once on the dirt floor and was still. Slocum took the gun out of her hand. He touched her face. It was dead to his touch. He picked her up and carried her outside and tossed her into the snow. He pushed her down and washed her whole body with handfuls of snow until she started struggling and the life came back into her.

X. Beidler found MacPherson's body the next morning at first light. He read the note and rolled the frozen corpse over to examine the exit wound. His face was untroubled and . . . interested. The faint tracks of the slow-moving sled were still visible. Once more he read the note. He thought about vengeance. He thought about justice. He looked at the clear blue sky and said aloud, "It will not snow today. The blizzard is over." When he mounted his horse, he urged it into a canter, though he wasn't a very good horseman and had trouble keeping his seat.

When he entered Walker's Saloon, he said simply, "Mr. MacPherson is dead. Everyone please gather."

While the saloon loafers raced around Blue Rock spreading the news, X. Beidler sat at a corner table with his hands folded in front of him and smoked a cigar.

MacPherson's foreman closed the Britannia. MacPherson's hostler brought all the mine's good horses into town and tied them up in front of the saloon. Other men who owned horses brought them and tied them up, too. The main street of Blue Rock, Montana, was lined with horses. Some of them were good horses; some were pretty sad.

Inside, the miners yelled and hollered. X. Beidler smoked his cigar. When he decided the crowd was big enough, he climbed onto a table. He stood until everyone quieted down.

"I have proof," he said. "Your boss, Pharoah Mac-Pherson, was murdered by John Slocum with his Sharps rifle. John Slocum killed him and stole the Biggest Gold Nugget in the World. It was found right here in Blue Rock, Montana. John Slocum didn't bury Pharoah MacPherson. He left him in a tree like savages do. He thinks you are too slow and stupid to catch him. He has contempt for you. He thinks you are gutless and less than men."

The miners roared. A few showed their teeth like wolves.

When they thundered out of town, heaven help anyone who stood in their way.

10

Despite the bad weather, they couldn't stay in that soiled, spattered, death-choked cabin that night. Slocum wrapped Lucia MacPherson in a blanket and sat her by the fire while he scouted around outside. About 20 yards from the cabin door, he found a small, open-ended woodshed. It'd do the trick, though they'd miss the comfort of a fire.

The blizzard had stopped. Through holes in the scudding clouds, Slocum could see the bright, indifferent stars. The wind was working the surface snow and skimming the snowbanks, hurling icy particles at Slocum's shins and ankles. No matter.

In the woodshed, he found a bucket of square-cut nails and the rusted head of a hammer. He tacked some of the Indian robes over the open end of the shed and across the ill-fitting plank walls. He chopped a mass of pine boughs for their bed and interlaced them so they'd stay springy through the night. He spread a few more buffalo robes across the boughs. It'd do.

The cabin stank like a killing floor. Lucia was staring into the fire. It was quiet. Just the noise of the fire, the tiny sighs and grunts of George Ives's belly, already filling up with death gases. Slocum pulled his collar up. Lucia let him bundle her up and lead her like a sleepy child.

They wrapped themselves in the buffalo robes. Slocum was ready for a little shut-eye, but Lucia lay beside him stiff as a board, thinking whatever she was thinking. She felt cold against his arm. The wind was hurling little shards of ice against the woodshed's walls, but under the robes they were snug enough. Lucia's breathing was quick and regular.

After half an hour of silence, she said, "They were . . . asking for it, weren't they?"

"Beggin' for it."

He felt her shake her head up and down. She said, "John, I feel so dirty. I feel so dirty." And she rolled over on top of him and guided him into her with her hands and they lay still and joined for a very long time until he felt the last of the meanness pouring out of her and she bit her lip hard and cried.

In the morning, Slocum got himself up, though she reached for him, half asleep, and didn't want to let him go. "John? John?"

"I'm here," he said, and knelt to stroke her forehead. She muttered something he couldn't make out and fell back into her slumber.

The horses' breath was steaming in the bright, bitterly cold air. Slocum took his time feeding them because he enjoyed caring for horses and liked watching them eat. So industrious. So single-minded.

About the time Slocum was feeding the horses, X. Beidler had returned to the spot where he found Pharoah MacPherson's body. But, of course, Slocum didn't know that.

Once the horses were grained up, Slocum started one chore he didn't care for. He backtracked Sheriff Hammer into the woods where he and George had ambushed the Blackfeet. The two men had spent time in a clearing just south of the cabin. Time enough for an Indian family, anyway.

The bodies were iced over, and the pools of blood under the neck wounds had frozen. One by one, he dragged the bodies back to the cabin. He took the man first, since he was the heaviest. He dragged the little girl last. He didn't arrange the bodies at all. They were frozen, and he didn't feel like thawing them just so he could lay them out in a more dignified posture than the arm-outstretched, belly-clutching postures they'd found themselves murdered in. The girl's eyes were open and white with ice. Slocum wished he could close them, but he couldn't. He took off his hat and muttered what he remembered of the Blackfoot mourning chant—that high, keening lament that's usually sung by the youngest and oldest women. It didn't take him long, since he didn't remember all of it. He plucked the London Colts off the floor before he shut the door and fired the cabin.

Lucia was up and dressed in her heaviest clothes. She greeted Slocum cheerfully, like she'd put all the events of last night behind her, and Slocum supposed that she had. She squinted against the bright sunlight and asked, "Well, John, where to?"

Slocum shrugged. "Not Blue Rock."

With Lucia at the reins and Slocum hauling on the lead traces, they made poor time through the snow. It had drifted since last night, and last night there'd been two men hauling on the traces. The horses didn't know what their hooves were hitting under the snow crust, and their fetlocks were balls of ice. The lead Morgan got cranky, and Slocum had his hand wrapped in the leathers and was shouting and cajoling and tugging and heaving. His boots were stuffed with snow, his pants were frozen to his legs, and he didn't like stumbling in the snow any better than the horses did.

Lucia was working the stockman's whip—just a *pop* beside a horse's ear to move it in or out, another *pop* to get the leader's attention. Slocum and Lucia helped the team keep its footing and balance and they were working as one unit: two humans, four animals.

Finally, they floundered over a snow hummock, the slope dropped away, and the Blue Rock Trail lay dead ahead.

It was tricky work easing that heavy sled off the bank onto the trail, and when they managed it, Slocum patted the lead Morgan's heavy neck. He and that horse were starting a fine relationship. He sat on the seat beside Lucia, pulled off his boots and emptied the snow. He took his socks off and squeezed them dry. "Whoooee!" he said. The clear air and the snow-capped peaks bounced his "whooee" right back at him.

Lucia looked at the leathery, grinning, weather-beaten face beside her and had to laugh out loud. She was alive. It was a glorious day and she was *alive*.

"What do you want to do with the gold?" she asked.

"Don't ask."

"Really, what can we do with it?" She turned to look at the tarp-covered rock they'd hauled so far. "I wonder," she mused. "I wonder if Queen Victoria really *cares* about this rock."

Slocum lit a smoke. "Probably doesn't even know it's comin'," he said.

"But what would we do with it?" Lucia's eyes were puzzled, but the laugh hadn't left the corners of her mouth.

"Expect we could sell it. Beat it up small enough and it wouldn't be a nugget anymore. It'd just be half a million in gold."

"It is *very* ugly."

"Yep."

"Would it be hard to get to Denver?"

Slocum thought. "I reckon there's one or two boys between here and Colorado who'd kill their own mothers for it."

Lucia discarded her laugh and put on her proud face. "Are they any tougher than Sheriff Hammer? Or George Ives?"

"They weren't tough. They were just mean."

"I suppose you don't think I can help protect it?"

Slocum was thinking of men like Frank Dalton and Texas John Slaughter and the Sundance Kid. He was thinking of Lucia MacPherson's courage. "Beidler'll be after us as soon as he finds that note. He'll stick to us like a burr until we have a showdown."

"We'll stop him, too," Lucia said.

"He ain't the sort of man who'll stop easy. He ain't very shrewd and he's got a miserable tailor, but he'll keep comin'."

"Uh-huh. Are there any fine hotels in Denver?"

"A couple. The Drover's House is good."

"I want to sell the nugget and take the largest suite in the finest hotel in Denver and have them bring buckets of iced champagne and tins of *pâté* and caviar. Then I shall draw all the blinds and fuck you to death."

John Slocum laughed. When he stopped laughing, he looked at Lucia's lovely, dead-serious face, said, "Sounds like a good idea to me," and popped his whip and they were on their way.

The snow cornice was like a half-roof jutting out from the sharp rock ledges above the trail. It weighed perhaps 50 tons. All winter it had frozen and refrozen. Its surface was slick, and the sun reached down to warm the rock the ice clung to. From time to time, with a loud grinding noise, the cornice would settle a couple of inches and a gush of water would burst out under its base to freeze solid again just a few feet farther down the track. When the cornice shifted, the snow motes danced on its surface and it went out of focus for a second.

X. Beidler and his 20 men were moving much faster than the heavy sled, and Beidler guessed they'd come upon John Slocum not long after noon. The sled tracks were fresh—no longer drifted over—and Beidler was smiling: a broad smile that looked like a slash in his pasty face.

The men riding with Beidler all had good horses. The spavined horses and the lungers and the poorly shod had dropped out. About half the miners had simply lost heart and pretended their horses had thrown a shoe or gone lame. They waved sadly as their comrades rode on without them. The stragglers gathered together in twos and threes to ride back to Blue Rock. When they got back to town, they headed straight for Walker's Saloon, where they gnashed their teeth and wished that their damn horse hadn't broken down, because "I would have liked to get me a piece of that Slocum."

X. Beidler had the hanging rope wrapped around his chest like a rough corset. The loop was over his shoulder and the 13 knots were already tied.

Beidler thought what he'd say to Slocum. "I believed you," he'd say, "but you betrayed my trust and the trust of the man you so foully murdered." He liked the phrase "foully murdered and kept whispering it to himself—"foully murdered, foully murdered"—over the beating of the horse's hooves.

The sun danced on the snow and it was like they were riding through a hall of mirrors. The sun flared in the riders' hair, and the horses' manes blew fresh and clean. The hooves were quick in the snow and not very loud. Their *thud, thud, thud,* taken together, sounded like a great wind rushing through the pine forest. *Like justice itself,* Beidler thought.

X. Beidler sang a song. At first he sang softly, because he didn't want his vigilantes to hear him, but after a while he forgot the others and, flying over the snow, yelled:

"For still our ancient foe
Doth seek to work us woe.

179

Strong mail of craft and pow'r
He weareth in this hour.
On earth is not his e . . . e . . . e . . . equal."

At first, Slocum thought he was hearing the distant rushing sound of an avalanche. Then he thought it was the wind. He was trotting the horses through a tunnel of trees, moving at a pretty brisk pace, though not brisk enough for his taste. But the sound got louder and it wasn't the wind.

"Oh, hell," Slocum said, and whipped the horses. Startled, they lunged into harness, and the sled skimmed along over the crusted snow, whipping between tall trees, past a great boulder, through a wide deer meadow and into the woods on the other side. Slocum drew up suddenly and Lucia grabbed the seat. She said, "What the hell?"

"Listen."

"I don't . . . I . . ."

"That'll be X. Beidler, I expect. After this little patch of timber, the trail goes up into switchbacks. The trail's blown fairly clear of snow, and you ought to be able to make time. Get as far up the switchbacks as you can. I'll stay here and draw their attention. If I don't catch up to you, you just stop. Past the switchbacks, the trail dips into the biggest avalanche track I ever saw. No sense chancing it. If they kill me, just break down into tears and explain how I abducted you and ravished you and used you for my own wicked purposes. They'll go for that. It's the way they think."

Lucia raised her stubborn chin. "No," she said.

Slocum said "As you please" and whacked the lead horse's rump, and Lucia went rocketing down the trail. *"Adios,"* Slocum said, but she was too far away to hear.

Slocum tramped himself a circle of flat snow just like a dog prepares a bed. He wanted sure footing when the time came. He spun the cylinder of the Colt rifle. Smooth as glass. He slipped a cartridge under the hammer, making six in all.

He stared at the woods on the other side of the

meadow. The sound of the wind was getting louder, and he squinted his eyes and strained his ears, because it sounded like some damn fool among them was singing. He could almost make out the melody. Some church tune, sung half a note flat. Oh, well, they were all crazy, anyway.

Slocum leaned the Colt against his leg and built a smoke. Last day; maybe last smoke. It was a real nice day. The air was bright and cold and bit at his nostrils and he stretched, feeling the muscles work under his skin. He coughed. His mouth was a little too dry to smoke, so he dropped his smoke in the snow.

John Slocum was standing just inside the screen of trees, planted dead center on the trail. The sun was bouncing off the snow into the vigilantes' eyes and they didn't see him, though they crashed into the deer meadow no more than 100 yards away. When he picked up his rifle, one of the vigilantes saw the motion, gave a tremendous shout—"Hey!"—and drew his Colt and fired. The bullet went into a snowbank about 50 feet ahead and ten feet to the right, but it was well meant. The shout and shot surprised Beidler, and he stood in his saddle to see what and who. A few more vigilantes had their guns drawn and were pumping lead.

"He's mine!" Beidler shrieked. "Leave him for the rope. Stop shooting!" More vigilantes were blazing away. They'd been excited by the gunfire. "He's mine!" Beidler screamed, though with the speed of the horse and the snow glare blinding him, he couldn't even see Slocum yet.

Slocum watched the rolling barrage of vigilantes and a smile flickered over his lips. He would have spat, but his mouth was a mite dry. *Damn amateurs,* he thought. He was in the shadows and they were in full sunlight. He was standing still and they were trying to shoot from atop wildly charging horses. The bullets buzzed by him and whapped into the trees. Some bullets threw gouts of snow in the deer meadow. One or two thupped by his ear close enough to make him think about accidents. Eighty yards. The rifle hung loose in his hands. He'd wait until they hit 50.

The black figure of the German was slightly in the lead, though it wasn't real clear whether he was galloping his horse or whether it was running away with him. He was just about able to stay aboard, bouncing like a sack of flour. Beidler's horse's hooves were throwing snow in the air, so the men in the rear of the pack were charging through a snowstorm, but it didn't keep them from shooting—no sir.

Slocum wondered if one of the men in the back would hit one of the leaders. He did hope so.

Sixty yards. The Colt felt ready, eager to jump up and speak its piece. The vigilante bullets were coming a little closer now, and Slocum knew he was pressing his luck. He thought about trying something fancy, like taking Beidler in the middle of the nose, but then he growled at himself, "Damn show-off kid." Fifty yards. The Colt jumped up; Slocum drew his bead on Beidler, but his finger locked. He couldn't pull the trigger. Sweat stood on his forehead. Sweat ran cold and swift down his arms. Forty yards. *Thup, thup*—right past his ear.

And then Slocum's Colt spoke. It fired six shots, and John Slocum didn't have any idea what he'd shot or why he'd decided until the horses started going down. He let the rifle sag. He wouldn't have time to reload, anyway. He cursed himself and the promise that had forced his hand, and the tears came to his eyes as six fine horses died.

A horse doesn't die all at once, even with its skull gone or a shot through its heart. It runs on for a bit until it overruns its own legs. The rider goes on over its head. The horses that fell tripped up the horses behind them and two men were punched into the snow and one of them would never get up again. The horses piled up. The near riders reined back hard, and the riders behind them piled into them, and more horses went down.

X. Beidler was briefly airborne. His reins had gone

slack and unresponsive and then his horse was gone out from under him. Beidler hit a snowbank and it took the wind out of him.

Slocum swore bitterly, "Goddammit! Goddammit to hell!" He wheeled and trotted down the trail after Lucia. Damn, he hated to see a good horse die.

Beidler puked and gasped. A horse reared up over him, and Beidler rolled to get out from under the horse's flashing hooves. "You ignorant mucker," he yelled, "get away from me! Get away!"

It took a few minutes for the live horses to get untangled from the dead ones. It took more minutes to pull vigilantes out of the snowbanks and from under the horses Slocum had killed. One they didn't bother to pull out, because all they could see was his legs under the barrel of a huge dead gray. When they kicked at the legs, they didn't move.

"He's all smashed up under there. That damn horse must weigh fifteen hundred pounds."

"Yep. He's mashed, all right."

X. Beidler stared at the vigilantes who'd made these observations with such rage in his flat eyes that they found some excuse to take their observations elsewhere.

Beidler pointed to the three nearest men. "You: Get after him on foot. We'll follow as soon as we rest the horses. He won't be far ahead. That sled can't travel faster than a man can walk."

The three designated volunteers glanced at one another. "There's five of us on foot now," one observed carefully. "I count six dead horses and only one dead rider. Why don't we all go?"

"All right, all right. Get the hell out of here."

Beidler didn't give a damn about the horses. He didn't give a damn what happened to the men he'd sent after Slocum. He wanted to look into the white space of the distant white mountains and breathe real deep until he could think straight again.

John Slocum was dogtrotting along after the sled. He hadn't remembered the woods to be quite this deep, but the tracks went on straight ahead of him and he couldn't get lost. He ran easily, though he crashed through the snow crust from time to time. When he broke out into the sunlight again, there were six switchbacks climbing the ridge to his right. Lucia and the sled had negotiated four of them and she was standing on the seat, yelling for the horses to pull harder. Slocum started right up the ridge, taking a shortcut between the switchbacks. The switchbacks, top to bottom, didn't cover more than 500 yards. If you'd laid them out end to end, they would have gone nearly a mile. The ridge was very steep and Slocum's legs were pumping and the snow slithered away under his clawing hands almost as quickly as he could lift himself. Slocum had an image in his mind of a salmon swimming upstream. He felt like a damn fish swimming and grabbing his way up that steep ridge. If he stopped churning forward, he'd roll right back down, and if the damn trail didn't stop him, hell, he'd roll downhill until dinnertime.

The air was thin, and his lungs weren't working so good and the world was going black, just like an eclipse of the sun. His body was still climbing and his hands were still grabbing for every scrub brush that raised its head above the snow. A pair of hands grasped his wrists and held on.

"I'm all right," he gasped. He sat down beside the sled. He felt like somebody had been kicking him in the lungs while someone else was bleeding him. The path he'd made up through the snow looked like the track of a demented earthworm. He stood up. He coughed. "Let's make tracks," he said.

Slocum got hold of the Morgan leader again, and the big horse set its feet against the snow and heaved. They got moving. Only one switchback ahead of them now. Their outfit was almost too wide for the turn, and Slocum wondered how the hell Lucia had handled it alone.

Bullets started coming, but the vigilantes were far

184

below them, and they had some cover from the lip of the trail. Slocum was talking the horses up the last pitch: "Oh, come on, you sweet-natured son of a bitch, you bastard whore, *pull.*"

Slocum was real close to the Morgan when the bullet hit it. Just a *thump* and the change in the Morgan's eyes.

The switchback was just ahead, but this pitch was very steep. The Morgan was hit bad, but it was still pulling. Fire came from below, mostly wide of the mark. Lucia's whip was silent. She was beside Slocum, hauling on the traces, throwing her strength into it.

They were over the top now. The sled tottered and almost hung up, but they were in the clear now. A few shots were heard, then silence.

Silence, except for their heavy breathing and Slocum's coughing and the creak of the leather and a curious sighing sound the lead Morgan made. Slocum stroked the horse. The bullet had gone in just in front of the horse's hip. The entry wound was ugly and there was no exit wound. Probably the bullet was tumbling when it hit. It was probably a pistol bullet: .44 or .45. It was certainly inside the horse's gut cavity.

"She won't live," Slocum said.

Ahead, the trail ran around the lip of a plateau. On the right, mountain peaks rose a couple of thousand feet. The trail crossed an enormous avalanche track. Boulders big as houses, torn-up trees and roots—everything covered with this year's blanket of snow. The plateau lay below a V-shaped slash in the mountain, and halfway up the V, Slocum could see the biggest snow cornice he'd ever seen in his life. The color of the snow was bad: rotten.

That cornice would sweep the plateau sometime this winter sure as hell. Maybe today.

When he heard noises behind them, Slocum walked to the switchbacks and took a look-see. Beidler and nine of his vigilantes were plodding up the first switchback. His other men must have quit. In his dusty black coat, Beidler looked like a beetle: an undertaker beetle. The vigilantes looked diligent, careful, deadly and dull. They came on, inevitable.

The Morgan was losing a lot of blood and the blood was tinged with mucous. The bullet had torn something inside.

Slocum felt his anger grow. It grew very quickly, fed by the sight of the dusty band of vigilantes and the wounded horse. His anger became a grin; the kind of funny grin corpses wear. His eyes were very clear and very remote, like the eyes of a bird of prey.

"Lucia," he drawled, "it's gonna get rougher up ahead."

Lucia threw back her head, smiled a fierce smile and said, "That's all right. It's been loads of fun till now."

"I'm gonna have to kill those gents. You want out?"

"What a contemptible idea, John."

He nodded. He said, "Give me a kiss." She did. He clucked at the horses and they moved onto the avalanche plateau.

The trail wound around the old scars of the ancient torrent. It zigged and zagged and doubled back on itself. Slocum didn't rush the horses. The Morgan had something wrong with its gait. Lucia was humming "Drink to Me Only with Thine Eyes." The sled slipped through the boulders, rode around and over the tree trunks. The Morgan was definitely broken-gaited now.

I sure am hell on horses, Slocum thought.

The snow cornice towered above them like a white patch on the sky. It shimmered and groaned and creaked, and the loose snow on top of it would bounce now and again.

X. Beidler wasn't in any big hurry. He looked at his nine vigilantes and thought them good *citizens.* He liked the ring of the word. Beidler was bruised and wet and his pocket watch was broken. He'd smashed it trying to duck the hooves in the deer meadow. His father had given him that watch and it kept railroad

186

time. The glass was shattered and something inside rattled when he shook it.

X. Beidler didn't often think of himself as a pleasure-loving man. But he took pleasure thinking about Slocum. The weight of the rope around his chest was a pleasure, too. And the sun was warm and the air was pure. His clothes were too wet for any kind of fast draw, so he rode with his belly gun in his fist, resting on the saddle's roping horn.

Even though they were walking their horses, they made better time up the switchbacks than the sleds had. On the last pitch, Beidler dismounted to examine the first spots of blood. As he walked toward the top, the spots got bigger and bigger, and on top he found the pool of blood where the Morgan had been standing. Beidler knew it was horse blood, because there was so much of it. It couldn't be John Slocum's blood, he knew. He had to resist the urge to taste it to see.

One of the boulders ahead could probably serve as a gallows. Just find a flat one, snub the rope to a knob of rock and toss the man off. After prayers. He'd be allowed to say prayers, and if he wished to write a letter to his relatives, that would be fine, too. If he couldn't write or pretended not to know how, why, X. Beidler could write it for him. He'd had a little practice along that line.

One of the vigilantes was pointing. The sled. It came in sight for a moment before a twist in the trail dropped it out of sight again. The trail was so twisted, Beidler couldn't judge Slocum's lead. But it didn't really matter much.

The vigilantes were worried about the snow cornice that hung so heavily above the plateau. There was a coldness that hung in the air, a coldness that smelled damp and fertile, like newly plowed spring soil.

Beidler couldn't smell it. He didn't give a damn for avalanches. If his men would not go with him, why, he would go on alone.

X. Beidler was a very clumsy horseman. He was a

little pathetic on a horse. Maybe that's why the nine vigilantes followed him. They cursed, but they followed him. They certainly knew better.

The Morgan was foundering, blood spouting from its nostrils. Slocum forced the horse forward another ten yards to a high spot where he could see both entrance and exit of the avalanche plateau. He saw Beidler's vigilantes, but they were too far away to bother about.

The Morgan went to its knees, thrashing and tangling the traces, but Slocum was at its side, speaking softly: "Easy, you sweet-hearted bitch. Now, you just take it easy." He cut its throat. A two-foot fountain of blood spouted over him and streaked his face. The horse kicked once and lay still.

"I didn't dare chance a shot," Slocum said.

"You look like hell," Lucia said. "I'm sorry."

The vigilantes were following Beidler onto the avalanche plateau. They rode single file.

Slocum was peering at the end of the plateau. The river of shattered rock flowed under a small hillock where the trail came out. "It'll do," Slocum said.

He slashed the leather harnesses and freed the other Morgans. He transferred the Sharps .69 to the scabbard on the Appaloosa. With quick fingers, he unwrapped the blasting caps and set them on top of the dynamite case. Carefully he faced them toward the distant hillock.

"That's very far," Lucia said. She was pulling the tarp off the Biggest Gold Nugget in the World.

"I make it fourteen hundred yards," Slocum said.

The nugget gleamed in the sunlight, and the bullet gashes on its side were bright as sunlight on a painfully bright day. Slocum thought it looked very strange.

Lucia and Slocum doubled up on the Appaloosa. The surviving Morgans were tame enough but weren't saddle broken. The Morgans followed behind but not very far behind. No doubt they were glad for a little company in this lonely, spooky place.

Slocum couldn't hear the vigilantes, but he figured they'd have gained some. Two riders was a load for the Appaloosa, but it was a big animal. And it was earning its keep.

When they climbed out of the plateau, the hillock was much more bare than it had seemed at a distance. The snow was shallow on this windswept crest and the horses started pawing at it, hoping to uncover something edible.

"It'll be spring soon," Lucia said.

"I expect so."

Slocum slipped the Sharps out of its scabbard, found himself a dry rock and sat down. He was whistling something that sounded like a bobwhite's call.

Some of the vigilantes had paused to stare at the sled, but most rode right on by.

"They'll be emerging soon," Lucia said.

"Uh-huh. Too bad about the gold."

"What did we need it for?"

Slocum had a few answers he could have made, but he ran a dry rag carefully over the Sharps instead. He didn't want any oil shine to disturb his sighting. He picked out a clean bullet, inspected the lands and grooves and hefted several paper cartridges before he found one that felt just right.

When the vigilantes popped into sight again, they were much closer. They were galloping their horses.

When Slocum released the rear-sight tang, the thin ladder sight snapped up into place. He rolled the knurl until the notch rested midway between 13 and 14. "It's just a shade under fourteen hundred," he muttered.

Lucia shaded her eyes. "I'm afraid you'll have to be the judge of that, John," she said. "I've no eye for distances."

Slocum considered and then dropped the sight one more click and nodded. He glanced at the treetops. They weren't waving. No wind. Whatever slight cross-currents there were shouldn't affect a slow, heavy bullet.

The rifle floated to his shoulder and attached itself there. "Damn that glare."

"John, you just do the best you can."

The sled was very small. Part of what Slocum was seeing was what he was remembering. Just behind the front seat was the case of dynamite. It was about 12 inches high. The blasting caps were on top of it and centered.

Boom!

The Sharps has a hell of a kick, but this time it felt like a powder puff. The .69-caliber bullet took a good half-second to travel 1,400 yards.

The sled blew up. It became a column of flying debris. Slocum saw a gleaming streak that might have been the nugget, but he wasn't sure. A second later the sound hit them: the crack of the caps and the roar of the dynamite. Lucia shaded her face. A few very tiny rocks fell around them. The column was now a dust cloud.

The earth cracked. Slocum heard it crack. The ground twitched under his feet like a nervous cat. The tremendous snow cornice was shimmering like a strange white jelly. A sliver of ice broke off it. The sliver was 200 feet wide and 400 feet long. When it hit, the earth shook. The sliver made spume, just like a waterfall. The cliff disappeared in the spume as the cornice came down.

What had been solid became liquid. A river of ice 40 feet high poured out of the narrow V onto the plateau, carrying everything before it. Slocum saw 30-ton boulders rise and roll in the ice river like wooden bobbins.

X. Beidler was riding the best horse in Blue Rock, Montana. He was close to the edge of the plateau and far ahead of his vigilantes. He rode like he'd never ridden before. He became one with the horse for the first time in his life and they were trying, trying together. The hillock meant safety. It rose before him like an island. He rode hard, weaving through the last 100 yards.

No other vigilante appeared, though Lucia thought she saw a horse tumbling down the mountainside in the great white flow.

The very edge of the avalanche caught Beidler's horse and it screamed as the snow and ice smashed against its knees. The horse lunged twice before it lost its footing. Beidler jumped clear. He was just 20 feet from safety. Making curious swimming motions, he fought the flood, went under, bobbed up again and came a little closer. He found a spot where he could stand. Tiredly, he plowed through the shallow running snow at the very edge of the avalanche. He was 30 feet below Slocum and Lucia.

Beidler turned his back on them and watched the slide for five minutes until the last rumble died. Then he wheeled and marched up the hill. His step was firm.

He still had the rope around his chest, though half his coat had been torn off him and his holster was empty, his belly gun gone.

"Howdy, Beidler."

"Mr. Slocum."

"Got a cigar?"

Beidler fumbled in the remains of his coat. "They seem to be broken in half. Smoke a half?"

"Sure." Slocum tossed Beidler a match.

Before he lit up, Beidler looked at Lucia. "Ma'am, I presume you don't mind?"

"No, not at all."

Beidler stared serenely at the distant mountains. "Ma'am," he said, "I don't suppose you have a revolver you might lend me?"

Lucia's frightened eyes found Slocum's cool ones. "Give him one of Pharoah's Colts," Slocum said.

Beidler rolled open the cylinder, inspected the cartridges, snapped it shut and stuck the gun into the waistband of his pants. He smoked his cigar.

When he was finished smoking, he turned and said,

"John Slocum, I arrest you for the foul murder of Pharoah MacPherson." His pudgy hand hovered near the fancy butt of the London Colt.

Slocum propped the Sharps against the rock he'd been sitting on. He took the other London Colt and stuck it in his right-hand pants pocket. He spat out his cigar. He said, "I always like to give a man one chance, Beidler. Think on this: I ain't shot nobody in half a year. You'll be the first."

Lucia was saying something about no, no, this was a terrible mistake, Hammer and Ives had shot her uncle and . . .

Beidler's face had a sardonic look. He jerked his head at the avalanche. "How about the nine vigilantes under that snow?"

"I said I didn't shoot nobody. I never said nothing about blowing them up."

X. Beidler's eyes were puzzled, and then a strange glint came into them and the corners of his mouth broke and he started to laugh. He laughed until the tears stood in his fat eyes like crystals. While he laughed, Lucia was explaining, but the dusty little man kept waving her explanations away. "I knew," he said. "I should have guessed it, a man like you. It was Hammer and Ives all along. Of course it was. Of course."

When he laughed himself out, he offered his hand. Slocum didn't take it. The German lost a little of the color his laughter had given him.

Lucia brought up the Appaloosa. "So, Mr. Beidler. We'll be riding now. You won't be following us?"

The dusty little vigilante spoke very stiffly: "I have no business with the innocent."

As they rode on down the trail, Slocum was thinking they'd make an early camp. It looked like snow.